# SUMMER AT LOCHGUARD

## Dragon Clan Gatherings #1

## JESSIE DONOVAN

Mythical Lake Press, LLC

*Summer at Lochguard*

Copyright © 2021 Laura Hoak-Kagey

Mythical Lake Press, LLC

First Print Edition

Cover Art by Laura Hoak-Kagey of Mythical Lake Design

ISBN: 978-1944776299

**Books in this series:**

## <u>Dragon Clan Gatherings</u>

## *Summer at Lochguard* Synopsis

Join Finn and Arabella as they host the clan leaders, their mates, and their children from Stonefire, Skyhunter, Snowridge, Northcastle, and Glenlough. Not only will Finn and Arabella deal with a surprise of their own, readers will enjoy updates from some of their favorite past couples. Also, the clan leader mates have some mischief up their sleeves; Asher King watches as Connor MacAllister talks with his sister Aimee; and other little tidbits happen over the course of the gathering.

**NOTE:** This is not a stand-alone story. It features characters from *Seducing the Dragon*, *Healed by the Dragon*, *Aiding the Dragon*, *Craved by the Dragon*, *Winning Skyhunter*, and *Transforming Snowridge*.

The Stonefire and Lochguard series intertwine with one another. (As well as with one Tahoe Dragon Mates book.) Since so many readers ask for the overall reading order, I've included it with this book. (The most up-to-date version is on my website.)

*Sacrificed to the Dragon* (Stonefire Dragons #1)
*Seducing the Dragon* (Stonefire Dragons #2)
*Revealing the Dragons* (Stonefire Dragons #3)
*Healed by the Dragon* (Stonefire Dragons #4)
*Reawakening the Dragon* (Stonefire Dragons #5)
*The Dragon's Dilemma* (Lochguard Highland Dragons #1)
*Loved by the Dragon* (Stonefire Dragons #6)
*The Dragon Guardian* (Lochguard Highland Dragons #2)
*Surrendering to the Dragon* (Stonefire Dragons #7)
*The Dragon's Heart* (Lochguard Highland Dragons #3)
*Cured by the Dragon* (Stonefire Dragons #8)
*The Dragon Warrior* (Lochguard Highland Dragons #4)
*Aiding the Dragon* (Stonefire Dragons #9)
*Finding the Dragon* (Stonefire Dragons #10 )
*Craved by the Dragon* (Stonefire Dragons #11)
*The Dragon Family* (Lochguard Highland Dragons #5)
*Winning Skyhunter* (Stonefire Dragons Universe #1)

*The Dragon's Discovery* (Lochguard Highland Dragons #6)

*Transforming Snowridge* (Stonefire Dragons Universe #2)

*The Dragon's Pursuit* (Lochguard Highland Dragons #7)

*Persuading the Dragon* (Stonefire Dragons #12)

*Treasured by the Dragon* (Stonefire Dragons #13)

*The Dragon Collective* (Lochguard Highland Dragons #8)

*The Dragon's Bidder* (Tahoe Dragon Mates #3)

*The Dragon's Chance* (Lochguard Highland Dragons #9)

*Summer at Lochguard* (Dragon Clan Gatherings #1)

*Trusting the Dragon* (Stonefire Dragons #14)

*The Dragon's Memory* (Lochguard Highland Dragons #10, May 5, 2022)

*Taught by the Dragon* (Stonefire Dragons #15, 2023)

## Short stories that lead up to *Persuading the Dragon* / *Treasured by the Dragon*:

*Meeting the Humans* (Stonefire Dragons Shorts #1)

*The Dragon Camp* (Stonefire Dragons Shorts #2)

*The Dragon Play* (Stonefire Dragons Shorts #3)

## Semi-related dragon stories set in the USA, beginning sometime around *The Dragon's Discovery* / *Transforming Snowridge*:

## Chapter One

Arabella MacLeod stood next to her mate, Finn Stewart, along the edge of Clan Lochguard's main landing area and kept an eye on the skies for their expected visitors.

Their home, located in the Highlands of Scotland, was the first dragon-shifter clan to host a new tradition—the UK and Irish dragon clan winter and summer gatherings. And her mate had randomly drawn the right to host the inaugural summer event this year.

While some clan business would be done during the week-long visit, it was also time for all the clan leaders to relax with their mates and children, get to know one another, and hopefully form stronger ties.

It wasn't exactly what Arabella would voluntarily do, if given the choice, since she didn't relish being the center of attention. However, she took her role as a clan leader's mate seriously.

Even so, despite all the help she'd had from Aunt Lorna—her mate's aunt—and her cousin-in-law Gina MacDonald-MacKenzie, Arabella did her best not to pick at her clothes or shuffle her feet.

She'd come a long way from her little cottage back on Stonefire. Where, to forget her trauma, she'd holed herself up with her computer, staring at the wall filled with pictures of doors, wondering what her life might be like one day.

The future had turned out better than Arabella would've guessed back then. She was mated to a loving, sexy Scot, a mother to triplets, and was a female with more friends and family than she knew what to do with.

But sometimes, Arabella still struggled with her confidence due to the healed burns on one side of her body and the long scar on her face, both a result of a run-in with dragon hunters when she was a teenager. The injuries, along with being isolated for so long after her torture at the hands of the human hunters, both contributed to her occasional self-doubts.

Not to mention playing host to all the other clan leaders was definitely fraying her nerves.

Well, on top of what her daughter, Freya, already did on a daily basis, at any rate. Freya might only be two years old, but she'd been shifting into her dragon form for a while now and had a penchant for trouble.

Her inner dragon, the second personality inside her head, spoke up. *It's not the gathering you're worried about. Not really. You need to talk with Finn.*

*Soon. He has enough to worry about right now.*

*Why put it off? He should already know, unless he's too busy to notice his scent entwined with ours.*

Her beast was right—Finn should know her secret. And yet, he'd said nothing to her.

Maybe he'd been too busy. Or maybe he was waiting for her to bring it up.

After all, she'd told Finn three children was enough. They didn't need any more.

And yet, due to a series of circumstances, it looked like they would have at least one additional child.

Arabella should be ecstatic, especially since dragon-shifters loved children. However, she was barely two months pregnant and all she could feel was dread.

Which wasn't what a mother-to-be should feel.

She glanced up at her tall, blond mate, only to find him staring down at her, his brows drawn together. "Are you all right, lass? You're quieter than normal."

As much as she didn't want to hide anything from the love of her life, Arabella would wait to talk to him about her feelings and their future later, after their important visitors left. "Just a bit nervous. This is the first time Aimee will see her brother since coming to Lochguard. I hope it doesn't undo all the progress she's made."

Aimee King was their guest, originally a dragonwoman from Clan Skyhunter in the south of England. The female had been imprisoned and tortured as a teen under the former clan leader, her dragon silent ever since. Arabella had once had her own problems with her inner beast and had jumped at the chance to foster Aimee and try to help her. The younger female had come a long way from when she first arrived, but was most definitely far from wholly healed.

Much like Arabella had done before meeting Finn, Aimee kept to herself and didn't venture out very often. But it was reaching a point where Arabella was going to try and coax the female to attend a small event with others her age. Or maybe to help volunteer with the school, since she did well with the children she helped watch once a week.

However, all of Arabella's next moves depended on how Aimee did with her brother's visit today.

Finn rubbed her lower back as he replied, "Asher and Honoria will tread lightly, aye? But it's time for Aimee to see her kin again. And it's not like I could invite the pair here and bar them from seeing Aimee."

Arriving a day before all the other clan leaders,

Asher King and Honoria Wakeham were the co-clan leaders of Skyhunter, and also a mated pair. Arabella hadn't interacted with them much, since they lived hundreds of miles away, but Finn seemed to like them, and she trusted her mate's judgment. "Aimee did say she wanted to see them, but she wasn't exactly jumping for joy."

Finn smiled. "The only time she gets excited about anything is when she watches wee Freya. And that's only because our daughter could charm a leopard out of its spots, if she wanted."

Arabella looked askance at her mate. "And I wonder where she gets that from?"

Finn winked. "You love the both of us, so don't try to deny it."

She smiled. "Most of the time. Not so much when you try to charm your way out of scolding the boys."

He shrugged. "They haven't done anything worth scolding yet."

Arabella thought of the two-year-olds brandishing sticks as swords, going through the house, defeating "dragon hunters," which had turned out to be anything within reach, especially if it were breakable. "It's Dec's fault, mostly. Gray just follows along."

Declan and Grayson were the remaining two of her triplets, closer to each other than with their sister, Freya. "You only think that, lass. Gray is sly and acts when no one is looking. But he has a hidden rebellious streak at times." He leaned downed and whispered into her ear, "He takes more after his mum, after all. Why, just two months ago on that unusually warm day, you managed to lure me to the loch, pushed me in, and had your way with me."

She lightly pushed at his side. "I hardly think you complained."

He lowered his voice. "No, I was too busy moaning and getting you to call out my name as you came."

Her cheeks heated. Even after nearly three years of being mated to Finn, he could still embarrass her. "Finn, our guests will be here any moment."

"Aye, but they're not here just yet."

And before she could say a word, he crushed his lips to hers, her own parting on instinct.

Finn stroked inside her mouth, caressing, licking, exploring her as if it were the very first time all over again.

He pulled her up against his front, and she moaned as her hard nipples pressed against his shirt and firm muscled chest.

Threading her fingers through his hair, she kept his head in place, battling his tongue, needing her mate's touch, his heat, his taste.

She had no idea how long they stood there kissing. But when the wind started to crash against them, she broke the kiss to see two dragons—one red and one white—gently touching down in the landing area.

Arabella straightened her dress and smoothed her hair as she gave Finn a "look."

Not that Finn paid it any mind. The heat and humor dancing in his eyes said he'd gladly do more, if she'd let him, not caring if anyone was nearby. She whispered, "Behave."

He shrugged one shoulder, not at all contrite. After her mate winked at her, Arabella turned to see Asher and Honoria in their human forms, taking clothes out of the small satchels they'd been carrying. Once dressed, they walked toward them.

The pair were both in their thirties, pale-skinned, and tall. Asher had black hair and blue eyes, whereas his mate and co-leader had blonde hair and blue eyes.

Honoria's smile and eyes were warmer than Asher's. But Arabella knew his expression was a result of the male suffering for five years under his uncle's former leadership, which had unsurprisingly hardened him.

In some ways, she and Asher were alike—they'd both suffered unusual trials and had ended up with blond mates who possessed much cheerier dispositions.

Honoria spoke first. "It's nice to finally be back here. We haven't seen Lochguard since we visited for a few hours, just to ensure Aimee had arrived okay."

Asher nodded, and Honoria continued, "But thanks for letting us come a day early. After all the good things you've said about my sister-in-law's progress, I couldn't wait to see her again."

Asher finally spoke. "But only if she's ready."

Honoria gave her mate a look, as if saying they'd talked about this already. Not wanting the couple to argue, Arabella jumped in. "She *has* been doing better. While her dragon is still silent, she can tolerate occasional flashing dragon eyes and sometimes a dragon form. At least that's the case when it's with my daughter."

Honoria shook her head. "I still can't believe a two-year-old can shift already."

Since most dragon-shifters didn't start shifting until age six or seven, Freya was definitely a rarity. At least Arabella had moved past the heart-stopping stage of thinking her daughter would turn rogue and remain in her dragon form forever, which was what usually happened when a child shifted so young.

But no, Freya could change forms whenever she felt like it. Thank goodness her brothers hadn't figured out how to do it yet. Three tiny dragons running amok would most definitely give her a heart attack.

Finn snorted. "Freya will take over the world by age twenty, just wait and see." He motioned toward the path leading out of the landing area. "But you'll meet the wee rascal soon enough. Shall we?"

As they walked, Asher asked, "Is Aimee still staying with you?"

Finn shook his head. "Hardly ever now. She likes having her own place. Although sometimes she does stay over, if she's frightened from what I think are reoccurring nightmares."

Arabella noticed Asher's jaw clench at the mention of nightmares. He said softly, "I wish I could take them from her."

Considering the male probably had them too, from his own imprisonment, it only showed her how much Asher loved his sister. Something else she and Aimee had in common—protective older brothers who loved them.

Honoria squeezed her mate's arm. "Many who suffered under the former leader, especially those imprisoned, also have nightmares. I think everyone will for years, maybe always. But given all that Aimee endured, she's strong to come as far as she has. Not to mention the little girl I remember from my youth was always stubborn, like her brother, and I doubt that's changed." Honoria gave her mate a loving glance. "I have faith she'll come out of her shell eventually."

Asher looked uncomfortable, and Arabella understood him. Much like how her father had blamed himself for Arabella's tragedy as a teenager —when she'd been captured and set on fire by

dragon hunters who'd also murdered her mother—
Asher blamed himself.

It was yet another reason Arabella wanted Aimee
to become whole again one day—so that her brother
could be too.

Her dragon spoke up. *Just don't take him on as a
project as well. His mate can help him. You don't need any
more stress in your condition.*

Not wanting to think of the reason for her
dragon's statement, Arabella decided to change the
subject. "Come, we'll show you to your
accommodations first. Then I'll talk with Aimee to
prepare her for your visit."

Finn got Asher to walk with him and Arabella
smiled at Honoria. The female asked, "In your
honest opinion, do you think it'll go well?"

Arabella bit her lip and decided to share
something with Honoria that she might not want
Asher to know just yet. "I think so. There's a male
here that's almost a friend, which bodes well for her
progress so far."

The dragonwoman raised her brows. "What do
you mean by 'almost a friend'?"

"Well, his name is Connor MacAllister. And for
nearly a year now, he's stopped in front of her house,
did silly acrobatics to get her to smile, and then goes
on his way to work. A few times I've been there when
he visited, and she went to the front door to watch him

from there, briefly saying hello. That might not sound like much, but it's the closest she's come to wanting to talk with another male that wasn't a doctor or Finn."

The other female's eyes were searching. "Is he her true mate, do you think?'

Arabella shrugged. "I'm not sure. But from what Finn's learned, Connor knows she's delicate and merely wants to make her smile."

Honoria's gaze moved to the back of her mate. "Asher and his sister both need more smiles in their lives, no matter how they get it."

Arabella studied the female a second before replying, "Aimee works with Connor's sister sometimes, doing art therapy sessions. I was thinking of inviting Cat and her brother to dinner one night, with Aimee in attendance to see how it goes, but I didn't want to overstep my bounds."

Honoria shook her head. "You wouldn't be. However, let's see how Aimee does with Ash first, to judge if she can do the dinner. Although…"

"Hm?"

"Well, does this Connor come by her place every day?"

Arabella shrugged. "Nearly so."

"Maybe if she sees this Connor, relaxes a bit, and then Asher comes soon after, it might help."

Arabella liked how Honoria thought. "It could work, although we'd have to hurry. Connor walks by

Aimee's cottage at half past ten every day on his way to work. He all but runs the clan's restaurant."

Honoria nodded. "Right, then maybe we'll skip seeing our accommodations and head that way now? Ash won't like waiting in a bush or what have you until the male has gone, but I'll convince him it's the only way to see how Aimee is truly doing here, free of interference or nervousness from seeing us again."

Arabella smiled. "You're a bit devious. I can see why you're one of the Skyhunter leaders."

Honoria grinned. "I think we're all a bit devious when it comes to our mates, right?"

Arabella laughed. "Probably. Now, come on. We're both going to have to work some charm on our males to make this happen."

And as they went to convince their mates of the plan, Arabella's anxiety faded. Honoria Wakeham was lovely, and maybe over the course of the week, she'd make a new friend.

But as the males finally capitulated to their plan, Arabella pushed aside everything but the meeting with Aimee.

She only hoped Honoria's idea worked.

Oh, and that Asher didn't kill Connor for flirting with his sister, either.

## Chapter Two

Asher King crouched behind some shrubs, his mate on one side and the Lochguard leader on the other, and wondered yet again how he'd allow Honoria to talk him into this.

His dragon snorted. *This way you get to assess the Lochguard male without him knowing. You should like that.*

He mentally grunted. *I don't like the thought of any male near my sister. She's not fully whole and healed.*

*Maybe, but sometimes it takes someone outside the family to recognize what someone needs. This Connor MacAllister doesn't know everything that happened on Skyhunter and merely sees Aimee as a female in need of laughter and smiles. That's not a bad thing.*

He tried to think of how to say Aimee was too fragile for any sort of male when a young dragonman came down the path, carrying something in his hands.

The dragonman had dark hair and blue eyes and was probably in his early twenties.

Asher narrowed his eyes. This male could hurt his sister.

As if sensing his ire, Honoria placed a hand on his arm and squeezed.

The action helped to tame most of his plans of attack—at least for the moment—and he focused on the cottage in front of them.

Connor stopped in front of the two-story building and looked up. And there in the upper window was the pale, brown-haired form of Aimee, obviously waiting for him.

His sister smiled down at the male, held up a finger to say wait, and pointed downstairs. She then disappeared from sight.

In a few beats, she opened the front door. Connor remained in place, nearly ten feet away, even when the front door opened.

At the sight of his younger sister smiling and standing tall, Asher's heart squeezed a fraction. While she wasn't the fiery sister he remembered from before her imprisonment at age eighteen, she was no longer staring into space and ignoring the world.

His dragon said softly, *I know it's been hard to have her here and out of our care, but it's helped. That's all that matters.*

Before he could reply, Aimee's voice said softly, "Hello, Connor."

The male gave a dramatic bow and then grinned at Aimee. "Hi ya, Aimee." He raised the dish in his hands. "I made some cinnamon rolls." Aimee hesitated, and the male continued, "I can leave them here, if you like, and go on to work. But I heard you liked them from Ara, so I figured I could make some and see what you think."

Asher held his breath as his sister laced and unlaced her fingers repeatedly. She finally held out her hands, "You can bring them here."

He heard Arabella suck in her breath, but Asher focused on his sister. Somehow, he had a feeling this was the first time—at least to their knowledge—she'd wanted a male other than a doctor to approach her.

Connor casually strode up to her and placed the dish in her hands. He smiled down at her since Aimee was several inches shorter. He said, "It's a new recipe I'm working on, so if it's rubbish, tell me, aye? I'm trying to think of new things to add to the menu at the restaurant, and I need a bit of honesty."

Aimee looked down and lightly traced the dish a second. Every cell in Asher's body wanted to tell the dragonman to go, leave her alone, and not scare her.

But then she smiled up at Connor again and said, "Okay. I'll tell you tomorrow." She paused and then said softly, "If you come by a little earlier, I can tell you over tea."

Only because Asher was studying the scene so intently did he notice the younger dragonman's shoulders tense a second before he relaxed again. "I'd like that. I'll come by half an hour earlier. Will that work?"

She nodded and retreated a step back into the house. "You should go. I don't want you to be late for work."

Connor walked away from the cottage, gave another bow, and then waved as he dashed off.

As soon as the door closed, Asher turned toward Arabella and asked, "Am I right in thinking that's the first time she's done that?"

The slightly surprised look lingering on the dragonwoman's face gave Asher his answer, but still she nodded. "Yes. She's never invited someone to her cottage before to socialize, only if she needed help or if she has a session with Cat, or a doctor was scheduled to visit."

At her words, Asher debated what to do.

If he met his sister now, would it undo all the progress she'd made? If so, maybe it was best if he stayed away.

And yet, he wanted to talk with her and let their mother know Aimee was doing better. It'd been hard for their mum to return to Skyhunter after Aimee had first settled in on Lochguard, but it'd been best for all involved to give Aimee a true fresh start.

Even though it pained him, he asked, "Should I stay away from her for now?"

Arabella studied him a second and then shook

her head. "Aimee knows you're coming today. She's probably mentally prepared for this moment for a while, so canceling might hurt her more."

He swallowed, wishing he could merely be his strong clan leader persona in this moment.

But his little sister had been tortured and imprisoned, her dragon going silent, and right here, right now, Asher was merely her worried big brother.

Honoria took one of his hands in hers and squeezed. "It's time, Ash. You could wait five years and it wouldn't make this moment any easier."

He met his mate's eyes and took strength from the love and tenderness there. After a beat, he nodded. "Then maybe it's time."

As they all moved toward the side to approach via the path instead of jumping from the bushes, Finn said, "I'll let Ara take you two. Once you're finished here and settled by your assigned hosts, come find me if you need to. If not, you can relax and enjoy dinner at The Dragon's Delight. While technically it's Sylvia's place, Connor is pretty much in charge these days. The food's good too."

Asher met the male's gaze and knew what he was suggesting—they could spy a bit on Connor and his family.

Although spying wasn't quite the right word, more like Asher would gather information while getting to know some more people from Lochguard.

After all, if his sister decided to live here forever, he wanted to make sure there weren't any threats.

He nodded at Finn. After the Scottish dragonman kissed his mate and left them, Arabella turned toward him. "Ready?"

Taking a deep breath, Asher squeezed Honoria's hand in his. "As ready as I'll ever be."

"Just act normal and not be too overprotective. Aimee's earned a measure of freedom here, and I think that has helped most of all."

Arabella's words were probably true, although not being protective of his sister would be like trying not to breathe.

His dragons spoke up. *Use the charm you try to dredge up with the clan sometimes. That will help.*

*I suppose.*

He murmured for Honoria's ears only, "Try to keep me from pushing her too far."

His mate looked at him quizzically. "I think you'll do fine. But letting you know when you're being an idiot is sort of my specialty."

He snorted and Honoria grinned at him.

Leave it to his mate to make him feel better without even trying.

They stopped at Aimee's front door and Arabella knocked.

Time slowed, and despite it being mere seconds, it felt as if hours had passed before the door opened partway, revealing one of Aimee's hazel eyes.

Arabella smiled. "Hi, Aimee. Your brother and sister-in-law are finally here, like I mentioned they would be yesterday. We can go for a walk, or we can come in. Whatever works best for you."

Aimee opened the door a little more, until her entire face showed. Her gaze fixated on Asher.

The last time he'd seen her, she'd always had a vacant look, one that almost tried to pretend the world didn't exist.

This time, however, her eyes were searching and observant.

Even such a small change and improvement made him want to hug Aimee tight.

Still, he ignored the urge. Touch had set off screaming and nightmares before she'd come to Lochguard, and he wouldn't risk it.

Aimee finally said, "Hello, Ash."

Honoria still had his hand in hers and she squeezed.

He returned the gesture, taking comfort from his mate's presence and smiled. "Hi, Aims. I hope it's okay I came to visit."

Asher held his breath as he waited for an answer. She soon bobbed her head, stood back, and gestured inside. "Come in."

Arabella went in first. "Where to? The kitchen?"

"Yes."

He let Honoria enter the cottage before him.

Once he stepped inside, he paused a second to smile at his sister. "I'm so happy to see you."

Her cheeks flushed and she whispered, "Me too."

It didn't bother him that she seemed to be speaking the bare minimum. Bloody hell, he was ecstatic that she could speak at all, considering her near-catatonic state back then and Honoria had taken over the leadership of Clan Skyhunter.

She looked away, and he took that as his cue to follow the others down the hall and into the kitchen. Arabella had already filled the electric kettle and turned it on. Sitting on the counter was the container with Connor's cinnamon rolls. He wanted to ask about the male, what Aimee thought of him, would he hurt her, and any number of other questions, but he somehow managed to keep his mouth shut.

One of the things he'd learned quickly as clan co-leader had been when to talk and when to remain silent.

Aimee rushed into the room and went about getting tea things ready. Arabella spoke up. "Maybe after tea you can take Asher and Honoria to see where you volunteer with the children."

He wanted to fire off a barrage of questions, to learn more about what his sister's life was like here in Scotland.

However, he needed to hold back and wait for her to tell him things in her own time.

Which he didn't like one bit.

Aimee finally leaned against the counter. "Only if they want to go see the children. It's not that exciting."

Honoria smiled over at Aimee. "Oh, I'd love to see it. We're always looking for new ways to improve the clan, after all. That's part of the reason we're here, to see how a different clan runs."

He waited to see if the mention of improving Skyhunter would trigger a reaction.

But after a few beats, Aimee said, "I don't know much beyond what I do with my group of children, but I'm sure my supervisor can answer your questions."

Arabella filled in the information Asher was dying to know. "Yes, Aimee has been helping with the toddlers once a week. They seem to listen to her. I should know since my three rascals are part of the group and cause all sorts of trouble."

Aimee shrugged just as the kettle clicked off.

Instead of adding to the conversation, she went about pouring the water.

Honoria sought out his gaze and smiled at him. He nodded back, letting her know he was just as happy as her about how well Aimee was doing.

And even though his sister still never said much and almost never more than a few sentences at a time, it was clear that Lochguard had done Aimee a world of good.

Just knowing that lifted a massive weight off his

shoulders. Asher had felt extremely guilty at sending her away, but clearly it'd been the best choice.

Even if it meant she'd attracted the notice of one Connor MacAllister.

Maybe Asher would have to go spy on the male, after all, just to be safe.

## Chapter Three

E arly the next morning, Lorcan Todd glided the last mile toward Lochguard's main landing area, his mate flying at his side, and did his best to contain his excitement.

While he was looking forward to seeing all the clan leaders in person instead of via video conferences, there was a much bigger reason for his good mood.

He only hoped the others received his news with the same sort of enthusiasm.

His inner dragon spoke up. *We've been in charge of Northcastle for a long time. Adrian is more than ready to take over the leadership.*

It was true—Adrian Conroy had won the secret clan leader trials a week ago. He and Adrian had debated over whether the other male should come in Lorcan's stead to this gathering or not, but Lorcan thought it best to announce his retirement to the others in person. That way he could share his good opinion of the lad who would replace him, as well as give proper goodbyes to all of the leaders and ask for their continued alliances.

Especially as the three dragon clans in the south, in the Republic of Ireland, slowly passed muster by the Irish DDA and began their own clan leader trials to replace those who had been killed and/or involved in other scandals.

Since Northcastle was the only dragon clan in Northern Ireland, he and Adrian would need their British dragon alliances more than ever, in case chaos erupted again on the Isle of Ireland.

His dragon spoke up. *They won't turn tail because of a change in leadership. Some have worked with Adrian before, including the head Protectors on Lochguard. All will be well.*

*I hope so. Still, it's good our mate is from Clan Glenlough, which gives us at least one solid alliance from the Irish clans in the south.*

His mate, Caitlin O'Shea Todd, was the mother of Teagan, Glenlough's female clan leader.

Although he and Caitlin had mated not long ago —late in life—Lorcan looked all the more forward to his retirement so he could spend time with his sexy, loving mate.

As he and his female reached the main landing area, they received a signal from one of the Protectors nearby, and they each gently laid their satchels on the ground before touching rear legs to the earth.

Lorcan imagined his wings shrinking into his back, his snout shortening into his nose, and his limbs retreating into human ones. Once he stood in his human form, he turned to see his mate, Caitlin, had finished shifting as well, her long, black hair streaked with gray settling over her shoulders and a smile on her beautiful face.

He still had trouble believing she'd mated him. True, they'd had decades apart from when they'd first fancied each other as teenagers—not to mention they'd each loved and lost their mates during that time—but he treasured every moment he had with his second chance at happiness.

And now that Lorcan was retiring, he could truly spoil her and find some new adventures.

His dragon spoke up. *We could have a few adventures here. Maybe take Caitlin nearby and claim her under the stars.*

*That's hardly an adventure, dragon. I've done that often.*

*But not in Scotland. Maybe find one of those sandy beaches still warm from the sun. I'd like that.*

Not wanting to go down that road and have his dragon lay out a detailed fantasy, which would mean greeting Lochguard's leader with a cock stand, Lorcan ignored his beast and focused on his mate.

Of course he couldn't completely resist her. He took one of Caitlin's hands, tugged her close, and kissed her gently.

As his hand wandered to her lovely arse, she smiled. "Dragon-shifters may not care about nudity, but I'm not about to give anyone a free show, Lorcan Todd."

He grinned at her. "I'm sure it's been done before, love."

She shook her head. "Not by the likes of me."

Before he could reply, a young dragonwoman carrying a baby—or maybe toddler? It'd been a long time since his grown daughter had been that age— walked up to them, her curly hair barely contained with a tie. "Welcome to Lochguard, Lorcan, and Caitlin. We've met briefly before during Glenlough's clan leader trials, but in case you don't remember, I'm Faye MacKenzie, one of the head Protectors here." She raised her daughter's hand to wave. "And this is wee Isla. Say hello, darling."

He couldn't help but smile at the lass with her babe.

And even though his stepdaughter, Teagan, now had a child, Lorcan still had a pang of wondering if his own daughter would ever find a mate and give him grandchildren.

But he quickly pushed the thought away. He needed to focus on the individuals here and not on Georgiana. "Hello, Isla, Faye. This is my mate, Caitlin." Once the two females smiled and nodded at each other, he asked, "Have Teagan and Aaron arrived yet?"

Teagan O'Shea was the clan leader of Glenlough, one of four dragon clans in the Republic of Ireland. Only in recent years had Glenlough and Northcastle had friendly relations, largely due to the family tie between Caitlin and Teagan.

And that tie benefited Northcastle greatly since Glenlough's leader was mated to Aaron Caruso, a dragonman from Stonefire.

Aye, there were some complicated bonds between his clan, Glenlough, and Stonefire down in England.

Faye shook her head. "Not yet. Not only will it take longer since they have to travel via car with their bairn, but Teagan said she had a few things to do. Something about last-minute instructions for her brother."

Killian O'Shea had an even more complicated past than most. But he was Teagan's brother, who had briefly had amnesia and then lived with Clan Stonefire for a time. He currently resided back on Glenlough with his Stonefire mate, Brenna, and her father and baby brother.

Caitlin shook her head. "If Aaron can get Teagan to leave, it'll be a miracle. Ever since that trouble a wee while before, she doesn't like leaving her clan for long."

Lorcan put a hand around Caitlin's waist and squeezed. "Don't worry about your daughter. Aaron is one of the few who can get her to do something she doesn't want to. He might even be more stubborn than her, if that's possible."

Faye grinned. "There should be a competition sometime to see which dragon-shifter is the stubbornest."

Lorcan barked out a laugh. "I'd like to see that. Many a male would suffer a blow to his pride, methinks."

Caitlin rolled her eyes. "Females too. But let's hope our trip here is somewhat more productive, and we can do better than planning a 'stubborn arse' contest."

Isla wiggled, almost as if she were trying to jump in her mother's arms. Faye readjusted her hold. "That's our warning to start walking, so you'd better get dressed. I swear she has her father's sense of timing and punctuality."

Lorcan and Caitlin quickly put on their clothes and gathered their satchels. As they walked, Lorcan asked, "Where's Grant?"

Faye replied as she tried to get her daughter to stay still, "You're not the first to arrive, so he's helping with the Skyhunter and Stonefire leaders."

"Stonefire's here already?"

Faye shrugged one shoulder. "I think Bram and Evie wanted some babysitting help with their three children." She lowered her voice dramatically. "Or Bram just wants to annoy Finn whilst he still can."

Lorcan snorted. Finn and Bram acted more like

brothers during their conference calls, which meant they constantly poked, prodded, and annoyed one another. "You act as if they'll behave when everyone's here, but I doubt it. Not that I mind. It's a vast improvement over the old days."

Back when the clans had barely talked with one another, or worse. Relations between Northcastle and the Irish dragon clans hadn't always been as peaceful as they were now. It'd been the same with the other British dragon clans at one point too.

His dragon yawned. *Don't worry about that. Focus on the now and how once this week is over, we get to officially retire with our mate.*

Faye's daughter leaned to the side like a dead weight, obviously wanting down, but the dragonwoman shook her head. "No, Isla. You can't walk very far on your own yet. I have to carry you." She lowered her voice. "I wish you still fit in the straps across my chest."

Caitlin smiled. "Aye, you're getting to a difficult age. Although once she starts walking and running, you're going to have to be even more alert and watch her closely, especially if she's a curious one."

Faye sighed. "She is."

Caitlin chuckled. "Well, then you'd best start preparing your home now." She smiled wistfully. "It won't be long before my own grandson reaches that stage. They grow up so fast."

Faye nodded as she looked down at her daughter.

"Aye, they do." She readjusted her hold on Isla and added, "But to be honest, as long as Isla doesn't learn how to shift into a dragon early, like her cousin Freya, then I'll manage."

As Caitlin and Faye discussed babies and various stages, Lorcan merely walked with his mate's hand in his and reveled in the peace and normalcy of the day.

He'd had his fair share of drama, battles, and politics over the years.

And he was more than ready for calm, slower days with Caitlin at his side.

His dragon spoke up. *Soon. But first we need to survive the chaos of this week.*

*I can handle this week, dragon. Even if all the leaders are younger than me, I can hold my own.*

His beast preened a little. *Of course we can.*

Eventually they reached the cottage where they'd be staying. However, as soon as they approached it, the door opened to reveal a pale-skinned dragonwoman a little older than him. She had blonde hair with a healthy dose of silver, and wore a huge grin. "You've made it. Now, come in. Ross and I have everything ready, and once you're settled, we'll take you on a wee tour."

Faye spoke up before Lorcan could say a word. "Mum, let me introduce you first." She gave Lorcan and Caitlin an apologetic smile. "Finn thought it'd be a good idea to pair each leader with someone from the clan to ensure the highest level of hospitality. This is my mother, Lorna Anderson. Mum, this is Lorcan and Caitlin Todd from Northcastle."

Lorna waved a hand in dismissal. "Aye, I well know that. Now, come on. I have scones still warm from the oven, and if we don't hurry, my mate will eat them all. For a human, Ross has quite the appetite."

Before Lorcan could blink, Lorna had herded them into the cottage and right to the kitchen. A human male around Lorna's age stood with a scone in his hand.

Lorna walked over and lightly smacked his arm. "Don't eat them all, Ross Anderson. I won't have time to make more for at least a few days."

Winking at his mate, Ross took a huge bite. Lorcan somehow resisted laughing, and he could see Caitlin biting her lip to do the same.

Lorna looked toward the ceiling. "I sometimes wonder why I even bother." She pushed her mate away from the counter—and out of reach of the scones—before gesturing toward the table in the little kitchen nook. "Take a seat."

And as Lorna saw them settled—occasionally tsking at her mate for trying to steal more food—Lorcan relaxed. What Lorna and Ross had was what he'd soon possess, too—lots of time with his mate, enjoying the small things with nothing bigger to worry about than how to make Caitlin laugh, smile, or cry out in pleasure.

Aye, it should be a good week.

Provided Teagan showed up and didn't worry her mother.

## Chapter Four

R hydian Griffiths watched as his mate, Delaney, finished reading the latest children's book she'd written, one that hadn't been published quite yet, to a room full of both human and dragon-shifter children, and smiled at the sight.

Despite only arriving this morning after their long drive from Snowridge, his clan in North Wales, due to their young children as well as Delaney's still-early pregnancy, she glowed.

His inner dragon spoke up. *Of course. She loves reading stories to children, be it ours or others.*

*True, but I think it's more than that. I think her getting to interact with other humans is part of it too.*

Snowridge was about to have its first group of human females visit to see if any fancied the single dragonmen in his clan. It'd been a long process to ensure his clan was safe—being more isolated,

Snowridge had fewer interactions with humans on a regular basis—but he and his Protectors had finally felt comfortable enough to invite humans to their land.

And his mate was most excited of all, of course, since she was the sole human on Snowridge. Although as Delaney finished the story, her human friend Holly MacKenzie walked up to her and whispered something, and the pair smiled at each other. Holly was a human mated to a Lochguard dragonman, and the pair had first met back on Snowridge, long before his son Damien's birth. It was good to see his mate catching up with her friend.

His dragon spoke up. *There are several humans on Lochguard, both male and female. Maybe she'll make more friends this week, then you can stop feeling so bad.*

*Maybe, although I'd rather she not get too cozy with the males.*

His beast snorted. *Everyone is besotted with their mates, or so Finn says. There's no need to worry.*

Rhydian merely grumbled in reply.

To be honest, the human males on Lochguard mated to dragon-shifters—three in total—had been a surprise to Rhydian. He'd never heard of a similar human male-female dragon pairing on Snowridge, at least not in recent history.

Although if Holly MacKenzie's theories were correct, as Delaney had told him, then having human males mated to female dragon-shifters would help solve the uneven birth rate of more males than females usually found among his kind. Because apparently, a human male and female dragon pairing resulted in a much higher chance of a female child, more so than any other combination.

He resisted sighing and said to his dragon, *And to think we only have one human female on Snowridge, and that was a hard-fought battle. Trying to invite human males will irritate the older clan members more than anything.*

*It'll change soon enough. Remember, Lochguard and Stonefire have been allowing human mates longer than us. Maybe in two or three years, we'll be in a similar place.*

He hoped so, for the sake of his clan, which desperately needed some new blood.

However, as Delaney stood and finally made her way toward him, Rhydian pushed aside his worries about the clan briefly. The time on Lochguard was meant to be partly a holiday for them, and he planned to enjoy time with his mate.

As soon as Delaney reached him, he took her hand and pulled her to his side. "I think they liked the new story, love. And I'm not just saying that, either."

She snuggled against him. "I think you're right. I would ask the children point-blank, but knowing Rian, he's probably going around right now and telling everyone how brilliant it is, almost challenging them to say otherwise."

He spotted Rian's auburn-haired form moving

from one child to the next, animated as he talked. The boy was Delaney's orphaned nephew and their adopted son. And quite the charmer, when he wished to be.

Rian would be trouble one day, no doubt.

Rhydian chuckled. "No doubt Rian's chatting up your story. But I don't think even he's managed to convince them all of your greatness before your reading, since we only arrived an hour ago, and all the children were enthralled as the tale unfolded." He glanced to the side, where Fraser MacKenzie—Holly's dragon mate—sat with Rhydian and Delaney's baby son, along with Fraser's own twin daughters, all of whom were asleep. "Except maybe the small ones. However, if your story can put babies to sleep, then it'll be a bigger hit than the others, I think."

Delaney lightly hit his side. "They were asleep before I started, you bloody dragonman."

Chuckling, he kissed the top of her head. "So you say."

She stuck her tongue out at him, and he couldn't stop grinning.

He was just about to suggest they take up Holly and Fraser's offer to watch Rian and Damien—their youngest—for a bit when Finn Stewart and Bram Moore-Llewellyn, the leaders of Lochguard and Stonefire respectively, approached.

As much as he wanted some alone time with his

mate, he couldn't ignore the two males. The fact Finn had managed to get permission for them all to gather like this was a bloody miracle and not something Rhydian would ever take for granted.

He nodded his greeting at the two others, but it was Bram who spoke first. "That was quite the story, Delaney. Maybe I can convince you to stop by Stonefire on your drive home to share it with my clan. I know wee Daisy—our sole human child living there—would love it."

Rhydian frowned at the thought of adding another stop, possibly taxing his pregnant mate, but Delaney replied before he could. "It'd be nice to break up the drive, don't you think, Rhydian?"

His irritation faded to concern. "Are you exhausted from the drive? Do you need to rest?"

She smiled at him and leaned a fraction more into his side. "I'm fine, I promise." She looked at Bram and Finn. "Please tell me you're not quite this protective with your own pregnant mates."

Bram smiled, but Rhydian noticed how Finn paused a beat before grinning. Bram replied, "Oh, I was much worse with Evie, but she let me know where to shove it when I got too overprotective. Not that it made any difference."

Finn shrugged. "And Ara had triplets, so aye, I was overprotective. More than you can imagine."

Delaney sighed. "So much for helping me convince Rhydian to relax a little."

He moved his hand to her lower back and stroked it in slow circles. "You can more than take care of yourself when it comes to your right hook, but you'll never be a match for a dragonman protecting his mate."

Since Delaney was a former professional boxer, she didn't so much as blink at the reference to a right hook. "Good you realize that, Rhydian. Or one day I'm going to have to hold a boxing match with some of the grumpy dragonmen to prove my point."

Both man and beast mentally growled at that idea. Since he knew she was teasing—Rhydian had made it clear she wasn't to box anyone while she was pregnant—he focused on Bram's original suggestion. "We can stop by Stonefire on our way home, if you like. Carys and Wren won't mind watching over the clan for another day or two."

Love filled Delaney's eyes as she gazed up at him, and the extra day added to their trip seemed a small thing by comparison.

After he smiled back at her, Delaney looked back at the other clan leaders. "Then we can talk more about the details later, Bram. For now, I think I see my youngest stirring. And trust me, he'll wail like a banshee if I don't feed him soon after."

Bram grimaced. "Trust me, I know. It's why Evie is with our youngest back at the cottage and not here. My youngest son could be heard a mile away, I think."

"Maybe we should get them together and see if they'll calm each other down."

Bram shrugged. "I'm sure it's worth a try. I know Evie wants to get all the young children together at one point. Something about forming strong ties from the start."

Finn elbowed Bram playfully in the side. "Maybe wee Freya can teach them all to shift."

Bram sighed. "Don't even tease about that."

Delaney squeezed Rhydian's hand before excusing herself. Once she had Damien in her arms, she left with Holly. The human and her dragon mate were assigned to Rhydian and Delaney to ensure they had everything they needed while on Lochguard.

Finn spoke up. "I hear a group of sacrifices are heading to Snowridge soon, aye?"

Rhydian nodded. "Yes, so any tips you can share would be brilliant. I know it's up to the humans as to whether they find someone who suits, per the new rules, but I want to make it easy as possible. Not just to help my clan, but Delaney could use some human allies as well."

Finn slapped his back. "Aye, well, then come with Bram and me. We've learned a thing or two over the last few years and have some tips."

And as he headed to a small meeting room with Finn and Bram, Rhydian relaxed a little and absorbed all the information they shared. He'd been a bit hesitant to travel so far from his home in Wales, but Rhydian was doubly glad he'd come in the end. Not only had Delaney been able to see Holly, but he was also receiving information he could use soon enough. Far better information than what the Department of Dragon Affairs—DDA—had provided.

However, he still hoped for some alone time with his mate too. But first things first—Rhydian asked Bram and Finn every question he could think of, to better prepare himself and, by extension, his clan.

## Chapter Five

By the time Teagan O'Shea—the leader of Clan Glenlough in Ireland—her mate, Aaron Caruso, and their son, Kellan, were nearly at Lochguard's front gates, Teagan itched to shift and burn off some excess energy.

She loved her mate and son, but driving to Lochguard—as well as taking the ferry across the Irish Sea—had tried even her patience. Especially when taking the car meant extra days away from Glenlough.

Her dragon snorted. *Killian, Brenna, and Lyall will do fine in charge. There are no imminent threats, no challenges from the other Irish clans, and we have permission to be here.*

*I still don't like staying away longer than I should.*

*Think of it as a short holiday. Besides, Mam will also be on Lochguard and will want to spend extra time with Kelly, which means we'll get some alone time with Aaron.*

Teagan glanced at her mate, whose turn it was to drive, and smiled. *Aye, that will be nice.*

Aaron's lips turned upward. "Fantasizing about what's under my clothes again?"

She rolled her eyes. "Maybe I'm thinking about how you refused to ask for directions once we disembarked the ferry in Liverpool and how it added two hours to the drive because of it."

He raised a dark eyebrow and shot her a quick glance. "Liverpool isn't one of the friendliest cities to dragon-shifters, love. So no, I wasn't going to jog into a newsagents, ask for directions, and risk my family. Next time, I'll make sure we have a sat-nav with us."

In a rush to get out the door back on Glenlough —Teagan had kept finding things to address, until Aaron had forcibly picked her up and carried her outside—she'd forgotten to grab the wee bag with the navigation unit inside.

She sighed, especially since their mobile phone coverage was spotty over here and not a viable option. "I'm sorry I forgot it."

"It's nothing. Besides, I know you're just cranky from being cooped up inside the car for so long." He shot her another glance, full of humor. "And it's nothing compared to the final months of your pregnancy. I'm still on the fence about trying for any more children if it means dealing with that again."

She stuck out her tongue at him. "You try

growing someone inside you whilst trying to manage a dragon clan and see how you do."

He lightly touched her hand before putting his own back on the steering wheel. "I'll leave it to you. As you often said, us males would constantly faint from the strain."

She laughed. "That would be quite the sight, I must admit, you swooning for seemingly no reason."

"I don't swoon."

Before she could argue that maybe it was possible, Aaron finally pulled to a stop in front of the metal gates that had the word Lochguard entwined within them. A voice came over the loudspeaker, asking who they were. Once Aaron stated their names, the gates swung inward, and her mate drove inside.

As he parked the car, a sense of peace came over Teagan. After months and months of shaky relationships with the three other Irish dragon clans, it was nice to arrive at a place where she could trust every leader in attendance.

Even if she didn't know the leaders from Snowridge or Skyhunter as well as she did Stonefire, Lochguard, and Northcastle, Finn and Bram would never have invited them if they didn't trust the others wholeheartedly. Especially since everyone had brought their children and mates to this gathering, and Bram and Finn would cut off a limb before putting their own families in danger.

The pale, brown-haired form of Grant McFarland came out of the building and waved at them. Teagan hadn't seen him in person since the clan leader trials for Glenlough, but still, it was nice to see a familiar face.

She exited while Aaron tackled getting their son, Kelly, out of the car. She shook Grant's proffered hand and said, "Sorry we're a day later than we planned."

Grant dropped her hand and shrugged. "The fact you could get away at all, despite the distance, more than makes up for it." Aaron joined them, with Kelly in his arms. After Grant nodded to Aaron, he added, "I wish Faye and I had the time to act as your designated hosts, but as you can imagine, security is tight right now."

Aaron grunted. "As long as we have a place we can sleep and shower, I'll be happy."

Grant motioned for them to follow him into the Protector's main building. "Oh, aye, you'll have that. Although finding someone who doesn't have a wee one to keep your family up all night was quite the task. But Sylvia and Jake's daughter is old enough to sleep through the night and is usually well-behaved if her dad's nearby."

Teagan frowned as she tried to place the names. "Have I met them before?"

"No, but there's a reason I'm entrusting you to them. Jake Swift's cousin is not only mated to an

American dragon clan leader, but the same cousin also works for the American Department of Dragon Affairs. We've been slowly trying to get to know Clan PineRock—the American clan—and thought you might like the chance to do so as well."

She grinned. "You've put a lot of thought into this. You might've been a politician or diplomat in another life, Grant."

Grant shook his head. "No, thank you. I merely strive to do whatever I can for my daughter's future." He looked over at Teagan's son. "I'm sure you understand."

Teagan couldn't help but look down at her sleeping son too. "I do."

Grant reached a door, knocked, and entered. Teagan and Aaron followed. Inside was a couple a little older than her and Aaron. The female was a pale-skinned dragon-shifter with dark hair and blue eyes. The man was human and even paler, with ginger hair and a close-cut beard. The human held a wee girl in his arms that looked quite a bit like him.

The male smiled and spoke first, his accent clearly American. "You must be Aaron and Teagan. Nice to meet you. I'm Jake Swift, this is my mate, Sylvia, and this mini-me is our daughter, Sophie."

Once she'd introduced her family, she said, "I think you might be the first American I'll get to talk to for more than a few minutes. We occasionally get tourists near Glenlough or in Letterkenny, but never to our clan itself."

The female smiled warmly and finally spoke up, her accent marking her as Scottish. "Aye, Jake will talk for more than a few minutes, you can be sure of that." Sylvia lowered her voice into a mock whisper. "Although watch out for his American cockiness. I mean confidence."

As the dragonwoman winked at her mate, Teagan could see how much the pair loved each other.

Jake put an arm around Sylvia, kissed her briefly, and then looked back over at Teagan and Aaron. "And I have no qualms about showing affection whenever and wherever, much to Sylvia's chagrin."

Aaron sighed. "I wish I could say the same." Jake gave him a curious look, and Aaron added, "We'll have plenty of time to go into the lingering misogyny of older dragon-shifters and how much harder Teagan has to work to prove she's a good leader."

Jake gave a look of sympathy. "There's a female leader for a clan near my cousin's home, and I've heard stories. The struggle's not just in Ireland, it seems."

Teagan was eager to ask more about this other female leader—they were few and far between—but her son stirred, and she knew the signs well enough to know he was going to cry soon if she didn't feed him. "You'll have to tell me more later. But right now, we need to get Kelly settled before his tiredness catches up to him and he turns cranky. It's been a long trip."

Sylvia nodded and motioned toward the door. "Come with us, aye? We'll get you two fed, as well as the bairn. One of the benefits to staying with us is that I own Lochguard's restaurant, so we can get you whatever you want, nearly whenever you want."

And as she and Sylvia talked about food and what they'd both found their children liked so far, Teagan felt just like any other female for a change instead of a dragonwoman constantly weighing her actions and how they'd be perceived by her clan.

The friendly chatter relaxed her, and Teagan finally acknowledged how much she'd needed this time away.

Glancing briefly to where Aaron walked with Jake, she could also see the upside to forming ties.

She'd felt so alone with the recent chaos in Ireland between all the dragon clans, even with Aaron and her family at her back. However, right here, right now, she realized how she wasn't as alone as she'd always thought she was.

And for the remainder of her time on Lochguard, Teagan was determined to make the most of it.

## Chapter Six

Bram Moore-Llewellyn would entrust Finn Stewart with his life, if it came to it. However, as he and his mate, Evie, watched some of Lochguard's clan members carry away his children, he struggled not to charge after them and ensure they were safe.

His dragon snorted. *Layla was Gregor's protege and is also a doctor. And Gina and Kaylee are both related to Finn through mating. Our children will be perfectly safe with them.*

*Aye, maybe if it were only our three. But they're watching all the children of the various clan leaders.*

His beast sighed. *They have additional help, including Layla and Gina's mates, as well as the nurse Logan Lamont. Everything will be fine.*

Before he could reply to his dragon, Evie took his hand in hers and squeezed. "I know how much not being in control worries you sometimes, but don't let it ruin the night. Finn went to a lot of trouble to have this 'date night' for all of the leaders."

He glanced down at his beautiful, dark-auburn-haired mate and squeezed her hand in his. "I know, but…"

She smiled at him. "But even with three children now, you still can't believe you have a family at all? And you're afraid to let them out of your sight?"

Before meeting Evie Marshall—his true mate—Bram had been told he probably couldn't have children. Even though he'd been mated and a father for years now, he still treasured his mate, sons, and daughter every day and would never take them for granted. "You know me too well, love."

Standing on her tiptoes, Evie kissed him quickly before saying, "I should hope so." She tugged his hand. "Now, come on. At this rate, we'll be the last ones to the restaurant."

As they walked the short distance to The Dragon's Delight—Lochguard's sole restaurant—he released Evie's hand to put an arm over her shoulder and tugged her against his side.

Having his mate close was a simple thing, and yet Bram didn't have as much time as he'd like to simply hold his female. Being clan leader was an essential part of who he was, but it wasn't always easy to balance his family and his responsibilities.

His dragon spoke up. *Then make sure to enjoy the night to the fullest extent, and spoil Evie a little.*

They entered the restaurant and they both stopped a few feet inside, gaping at the scene in front of them.

Tables spaced apart were draped in white linen, with candles and flowers in the center. With the dimmed lights in the main room, it gave off a romantic air.

And that was before even taking in the soft music filling the room too.

Evie snuggled against his side. "It's lovely."

It was, and Bram would have to begrudgingly thank Finn for the night at some point.

Although it would irk him. He far preferred annoying Finn on purpose to get back at the bastard for annoying him more.

His dragon laughed. *Just stop. He's our closest male friend, and you know it.*

Not wanting to acknowledge the truth, Bram instead guided Evie the last few feet to where all the other clan leader couples stood waiting. Well, all except Finn and Arabella.

Before he could ask where they were, the pair entered from a side room. Seeing Arabella smiling and happy pushed aside Bram's annoyance at having to thank Finn for anything. The female had gone through so much, and the fact Finn made her glow meant the world to him.

Finn spoke up, and everyone turned at his voice. "I'm glad to see everyone managed to get away and bear leaving your children with my clan members. Whilst tomorrow will be a workday when we discuss clan-related business, we all deserve a night of fun and relaxation. If you're anything like me, you don't get enough time alone with your mate." He glanced down at Arabella, heat in his eyes, and her cheeks tinged pink. Once Finn gently rubbed his mate's lower back, he continued, "So have dinner with your partner. I'll do my best not to eavesdrop, although except for Delaney and Evie, the rest of us are all dragon-shifters, and we'll probably be able to hear every word. So keep that in mind, aye?"

A few chuckles rolled through the group before Arabella finally jumped in. "After dinner, though, we're going to play some games in the small event room." She indicated where she and Finn had just come from. "So no rushing off right after."

Finn grinned. "After all, you can ravish your mates later. Those watching the bairns are willing to do so overnight, for those who wish, as I'm sure they told you." He gestured toward the tables just as a few individuals—mostly MacAllisters, if Bram recognized them correctly from his previous visits—emerged dressed as waiters. "Sylvia and Connor MacAllister were gracious enough to close the restaurant for the evening for us, so be nice to them and their staff, aye? Now, let's head to our tables and pretend the outside world doesn't exist for a few hours."

Finn took Arabella's hand and went to a far corner. Bram looked to Evie, and she pointed to one near the window.

Once they were settled, a black-haired woman with blue eyes walked toward them. Evie's face lit in recognition. As soon as the dragonwoman was close enough, Evie said, "Cat MacKintosh! Given what I know of your mate, I'm surprised he's let you out so soon after having your bairn."

Cat rolled her eyes. "I'm perfectly fine. It's not as if I had Felicity last week or even just a month ago. Besides, my sister-in-law adores her niece and doesn't mind watching her. And since my mate trusts his sister, he couldn't argue me out of it."

She glanced toward a dark-haired human male across the room, supposedly talking with Rhydian and Delaney, but who was mainly watching Cat with a frown.

Bram couldn't help but snort. Lachlan was a human who also worked with the DDA and occasionally teamed up with his mate for projects, even if Evie hadn't officially been with the DDA in years. He said, "He's as bad as any dragonman. It's almost a prerequisite that any human male who wants a dragonwoman has to be like us."

Evie raised an eyebrow. "Any human, male or female, needs some stubbornness and backbone to be a dragon's mate. You lot are a lot of trouble sometimes."

Despite her words, Bram saw the humor dancing in her eyes. "Aye, but you must admit it's never boring."

Evie smiled. "No, I can't say it is."

As he stared at his mate, taking in her lovely eyes and face, he wanted to skip the meal entirely and devour her as his dinner instead.

But Cat cleared her throat before his thoughts could turn to what exactly he wanted to do with a naked Evie in his bed, garnering his attention. "I know that look, and Finn says none of that until later." She handed them each a piece of paper. "We created a special menu for all of you, so take your time, and I'll be back. If you know what you want to drink, I can take that order now."

Since Bram was determined to keep a clear head the entire week, he merely ordered some sparkling water. Once Cat took Evie's order as well and left them alone, he reached across the table and took one of Evie's hands in his. As he stroked the back, his finger reveling in her warm skin, he said, "Since we agreed to not talk about the kids this evening, tell me the last time you worked with Lachlan? I've thought of having him and Cat visit, so Rafe could have some human company for a few days."

Rafe Hartley was the only human male mated to a dragonwoman on Stonefire. He also worked with the British Army—secretly, of course—to help with human and dragon operations. And while often a pain in Bram's arse, Rafe was loyal to his family and the clan.

Evie shrugged. "Lachlan consulted me soon after his daughter was born. He now has a sort of go-between position between human and dragon businesses. I thought it might be worth it to have him come down and see what he can do to help in that department since some of the businesses in the Lake District are reluctant to pair with some of our artisans, such as Dylan."

Dylan was Stonefire's silversmith and an all-around talented jewelry designer, who had been trying to get human shops to sell his goods for years to mostly no avail. "Maybe tomorrow, when I'm meeting with the leaders, you can visit with Cat and Lachlan to see if he'll come to Stonefire for a bit." He squeezed her hand. "Even if you can't come to the meeting, you're a vital part to making this trip a success. I couldn't lead Stonefire without you, love."

She beamed at him. "You could, but you'd be half-ragged and full of sexual frustration." She leaned closer and lowered her voice. "And we can't have that, can we?"

With his mate leaning over, Bram could see straight down her top. The sight of her full, creamy breasts sent blood straight to his cock.

His dragon sighed. *Are you sure we can't leave early and take Evie to bed straightaway?*

*No. As much as I want her screaming my name as she comes, there's too much to do this week. And tonight will be about getting to know the others better, once we've eaten.*

*Then we need to claim her soon. You were on the fence about leaving Eleanor, Murray, and Gideon overnight, but I think we should do so.*

*I'll ask Evie and think about it.*

Evie's voice interrupted his thoughts. "Do I want to know what your dragon is saying? Because given your look a few seconds ago, I'm sure it's some kind of trouble."

He grinned, pulled her hand up, and kissed the back of it. After lightly flicking her skin with his tongue, he lowered their entwined hands back to the table. "Let's just say my beast is making a good case for leaving the children overnight with Layla and the others."

"Given where we are and that Finn would never let anything happen to them, I say we should do it." She gave him a heated glance, staring at his lips a second before meeting his gaze again. She purred, "I've gotten a lot better at seducing a certain dragonman, after all."

He chuckled. "That wouldn't be hard to do given how you tried wearing heels and stumbling right at the beginning, thinking it would somehow woo me into bed."

She sniffed. "I thought I did a rather good job of hiding my stumbles."

"Not good enough." He leaned closer to her and lowered his voice. "But I agree—you're much better at seducing me these days. Although I may have a few tricks left to teach you."

She smiled and ran a finger over his forearm, the caress sending more heat through his body. Evie murmured, "Then I say we leave the kids overnight, and you can teach me something new."

At the thought of Evie naked and tied up, his cock stirred again. Only because he saw Cat coming toward them again did he refrain from making a dirty comment. "Aye, we can, and I'll teach you a thing or two." He leaned back and looked at his menu. "But we'll need energy for that, love. So we may as well eat and enjoy ourselves with our clothes still on until then."

She snorted and looked at the paper in her hands.

And as they ordered, ate, and chatted about everything and nothing in particular, Bram enjoyed it all immensely.

While he had hoped to forge stronger alliances with the other leaders during this trip, the time away also taught him how he should delegate even more to others back on Stonefire so he could take Evie out once a week to dinner or some sort of date. Taking the Dragon Knights down had taken up too much of his time, and he needed to make his mate a greater priority again.

He'd start later tonight, by allowing others to watch his children while he caressed every inch of her lovely skin.

## Chapter Seven

Honoria Wakeham studied her mate sitting across from her and couldn't decide if she wanted to sigh or kick him under the table.

Her dragon laughed. *Kick him. It's the only way to get his attention right now.*

Given how Asher watched Connor MacAllister and his mother walk from one table to the next, getting ever closer to where they sat, Honoria wasn't sure he'd even notice.

They hadn't managed to see Connor earlier, when she and Asher had eaten lunch. Her mate had wanted to repeatedly come back until they did, but she'd managed to restrain him, saying how they had their clan's reputation to think of. And a stalker co-leader who might, just might, threaten a younger male to a fight so he could scare Connor away from Aimee wouldn't exactly endear the others to them.

And given Asher's narrowed eyes as he watched the younger male laugh at something Stonefire's leader said, Honoria definitely thought it'd been a wise course of action to keep him from being alone with the Scottish dragonman for this visit.

For the moment, however, she needed to get Asher somewhat less hostile before Connor reached their table.

Her beast flashed an image of an idea, and Honoria smiled. *That might just work.*

Discreetly slipping off one of her shoes, she raised her foot until it met Asher's thigh under the table. At the touch, he glanced at her briefly before glaring back at Connor.

Determined to distract him—no matter how much her mate would probably get back at her later—she slowly moved her foot up his thigh, toward Asher's groin.

As she started to massage his cock, not only did Asher's gaze move to hers, she felt him hardening under her caresses.

When she pressed lightly, Asher sucked in a breath. "What are you doing, Ria?"

She smiled innocently. "Trying to get you to look at me for more than two seconds."

As she stroked his now-hard cock through his trousers, Asher gripped the edges of the table. His voice choked as he said, "You have my full attention now, so stop that."

More than used to Asher's orders and dominant tone, she did no such thing. "Hm, maybe if I hurry, you'll be nice and relaxed by the time your archnemesis arrives at our table."

She noticed Asher bite the inside of his cheek, probably to stifle a groan at her slow stroke with her big toe. After a beat, he replied so softly she could barely hear it, probably to ensure no one else in the room could. "We have to sit through games or some such later, remember? I'm not about to come in my trousers and spend the entire time trying to hide it."

Her lips twitched at the image of Asher finding pillows or some such thing to hide his crotch.

She paused her torture. "Then promise you'll be civil to *him* and I'll stop."

"I just want to ensure he doesn't hurt my sister."

Honoria softened her tone a fraction. "I know, Ash. But by all accounts, Arabella MacLeod finally made a full recovery from her ordeal once she mated Finn. Maybe Aimee will need the same, and Connor seems like a good bloke, at least from what I can tell so far."

Asher stared at her, his expression guarded. But for a second, concern flashed in his eyes before he pushed it away. "If he can't handle me, he's not worthy."

She bit her lip a second as she tried to think of what she could say to Asher. After all, he and his sister had been imprisoned and tortured for years, so she understood him wanting Aimee to find a strong enough mate to protect her.

But strength didn't always mean military might or fighting prowess. However, convincing Asher of that would be a tough sell.

She finally settled on, "Just give him a chance is all I ask. For right now, he's merely Aimee's friend. And I think we can both agree that she desperately needs as many of those as she can get."

Asher searched her gaze a second before sighing. He nodded. "I'll try." Before she could blink, he took her foot under the table and tickled the bottom.

She jerked and laughed, unable to stop it. As the table wobbled, she tried to take her foot back. But Asher grinned devilishly at her and continued for a few more seconds, until the entire room stared at her.

He finally released her foot, and she merely shrugged at everyone else. She stated loudly, "I'm ticklish."

A few laughs echoed about the room, and she grinned. Honoria didn't embarrass easily. And unlike Asher, she had no problem trying to charm a room.

When she looked back at Asher, he shook his head at her. She pointed at him. "You know I don't care if everyone stares. In the end, you're the one who gets embarrassed. So maybe remember that the next time you try to get revenge in public."

Mischief danced in his eyes, which was never a good sign. "So if I just mentioned how you couldn't keep your foot off my cock at dinner, you'd be fine with it?"

While she'd rather not have everyone know about her teasing game of footsie, she wouldn't let her mate embarrass her. She shrugged. "If you did, then I'm sure all the males here would want their mates to try the same."

A Scottish male voice interrupted Asher's reply, "Try what?"

As she looked over at Connor MacAllister and Sylvia Swift, her cheeks heated a fraction. The younger dragonman could end up being part of their family one day, if things progressed with her sister-in-law. And she'd rather not have Connor's first impressions of her as a cock tease during a special dinner event.

Her beast laughed. *So you* can *get embarrassed.*

*Hush, dragon.*

Asher spoke before her in a decidedly dry tone. "Trust me, you don't want to know."

Honoria sent a silent thank-you to Asher for keeping his mouth shut before she smiled at Connor and his mother. "Thank you for the lovely dinner tonight. I'm probably going to have to waddle to the next room, I ate so much."

Sylvia smiled as well. "It's mostly my son's doing. But I'm glad you liked it."

Honoria held out her hand toward Connor. "Then thank you, sir, for the grand meal."

Connor shook her hand and grinned. And even though no male could ever compare to Asher in her eyes and heart, Honoria could see how Aimee's head might be turned by the attractive young male. He released her hand before he said, "My goal is to eventually partner with other clan restaurant owners and see if we can come up with a side business, one that allows us to work with humans for special events. So tonight was a wee test to see if I could come up with dishes I don't normally make, ones everyone should enjoy, given the notes you sent Finn about preferences."

Considering the male was only in his midtwenties, Honoria admired the confidence in his tone and his goals. "You did well, I think. And I can pass on your contact information to the cafe owner on Skyhunter." She grimaced slightly. "It's been years since we had a proper restaurant, though."

Connor nodded. "That would be great, Miss Wakeham. Maybe one day I can visit Skyhunter and see about setting up a partnership to open a real restaurant for you lot."

Asher grunted, but Honoria continued to ignore her mate's grumpiness. "It'll be some months yet before I'd feel comfortable inviting outsiders. But as soon as things are settled, you're welcome to stay as long as you like. Right, Asher?"

She raised an eyebrow at Asher, and he reluctantly nodded. Even with his suspicions regarding Connor and his sister, Asher would love a proper restaurant on Skyhunter as much as she would.

It could also be a way to not only get Asher to better accept Connor, but if things did progress with him and Aimee, maybe Connor could convince the dragonwoman to visit.

Which wouldn't be easy, of course, given the dark memories Aimee had of Skyhunter. But Honoria held out hope that the female would finally return one day, even if only briefly.

Honoria exchanged a few more pleasantries— even managing to multitask and get her shoe on at the same time—before Connor and Sylvia went to the last table on their rounds. Given how everyone was either finished or eating dessert, she suspected they'd be moving to the other room soon.

So she leaned over, took one of Asher's hands, and squeezed. "Thank you for not being an arsehole to him."

Asher grunted. "I'm not saying I like him, but if he can get a restaurant going on Skyhunter, I might be able to tolerate him."

She rolled her eyes. "Males and their stomachs."

He gently tugged her hand. "There's something else that works even better when it comes to swaying my opinion."

As his gaze heated and his pupils flashed, her nipples tightened. "Later, Ash."

"Then I'll just have to whisper what I plan to do to you all through this evening. That way, even your dragon will let me be in charge when we're finally alone."

Her dragon hummed. *I'm not against that idea.*

As she struggled not to laugh, Finn's voice filled the room. "Now that dinner's finished, let's move to the other room, aye?"

Asher stood and offered his hand. Once he pulled her up, he brought her flush against his front and whispered into her ear, "Just know that I plan to torture you slowly with my tongue, bringing you to the brink, backing off, and doing it again and again until you beg for me to let you come."

A thrill of anticipation shot through her body, ending between her thighs. "Promise?"

He chuckled, and the sound turned Honoria soft. Her mate laughed more than when she'd first returned to Skyhunter after her years-long exile to America, but still not often enough for her liking.

After discreetly squeezing her bum, he murmured, "Yes," and then released her.

Honoria stumbled a second before finding her balance.

Placing a hand on her lower back, Asher guided Honoria to the other room.

Part of her wanted the entertainment to end early so she could have Asher all to herself.

However, another part of her wanted it to drag

on for hours so he could keep whispering dirty things into her ear.

Either way, she was glad they'd come to Lochguard. Too often they had to neglect their relationship to help the clan. But for a few short days, they could merely enjoy each other and remember why they were mates in the first place.

## Chapter Eight

The next afternoon, Finn struggled to concentrate on all the proposals, debates, and random teasing from the other clan leaders. Not because he didn't want to be there—the fact so many dragon clan leaders were in the same room together, willingly, was a massive deal—but because he worried about Arabella.

She had to know he could tell she was pregnant again. After all, his scent was entwined with hers, and he'd have to be an idiot to miss it.

And yet, she hadn't brought it up once in the weeks since he'd first noticed.

His dragon spoke up. *We're giving her some time to deal with the news. After all, it's a big deal. The triplets are a handful and stressed her out from the beginning.*

Finn knew that. And he'd been more than happy to only have three children. So when Arabella had asked him to get a vasectomy, he hadn't hesitated to schedule one.

The bloody problem was some disaster had come up, one he'd had to deal with, and he'd canceled the appointment. Even though he'd rescheduled, emergencies had kept popping up and pushing the date back over and over again. Until things became so hectic, he'd completely forgotten about the procedure at all.

Which had resulted in his mate being pregnant again.

Aye, he wasn't the first male to find himself with an unplanned bairn on the way, but his mate wasn't like everyone else's. Arabella was strong yet vulnerable at the same time, which was something he was always aware of.

And in their years of being mated, she'd never avoided addressing something so important from him before.

Which worried him.

If the clan leader gathering hadn't been scheduled and already confirmed by the time he'd noticed Arabella's pregnancy, he would've asked another clan to host it this time around.

But it'd been too late. And so, yet again, he had to focus on something other than his mate's well-being and happiness.

Which Finn fucking hated.

Bram poked him in the bicep, and Finn blinked. "Aye?"

The Stonefire leader frowned at him. "Were you listening?"

Even if it didn't show him in a good light, Finn had vowed to himself to be completely honest with the other leaders. "No, sorry. I was thinking about some personal issues I just can't seem to push aside."

As Bram studied him, Finn resisted putting on his teasing mask and pushing the other clan leader. For once, Finn just didn't have it in him.

Lorcan from Northcastle raised his brows. "If it's to do with your family, lad, then we can finish this later."

Since the Northcastle male was much older—his parents' age, if they had still been alive—he let the lad comment slide.

However, before he could reply, Teagan jumped in. "I agree with Lorcan. We'll all be in Lochguard for at least four more days. There's no reason to try and get everything crammed into one meeting. We've been at it for hours already as it is."

The others murmured their agreement. Whether because they wanted a break or because they were trying to tell Finn it was okay to deal with personal issues, he had no idea.

But Rhydian from Snowridge stood, garnering everyone's attention. "I think a break is a brilliant idea. Delaney's morning sickness has started up in the last few days, and I'd like to check on her and see if it's gotten worse or better."

Teagan stood next. "And I wouldn't mind some time with my son, either." She flashed Finn a smile. "I think postponing the rest of the agenda until tomorrow would be grand, aye?"

Bram squeezed Finn's shoulder. "Go deal with whatever is the problem, Finn. Everyone here knows how hard it is to balance a family and clan. And I'm sure I speak for the others when I say I don't want to be part of the strain placed on your family."

Everyone murmured their consent.

Finn bobbed his head, almost stunned by all their understanding. "We'll have a working lunch tomorrow, here again. Aye?"

They all agreed and slowly dispersed, except for Bram. Once they were alone, Stonefire's leader asked, "Does it have to do with Arabella? I noticed she's pregnant again."

All male dragon-shifters could scent when a female carried a dragonman's bairn. Still, Finn had been so worried about his mate he hadn't really thought about how the other male leaders had to know his situation. And even with Teagan, no doubt her mate, Aaron, had told her the news.

Probably the whole bloody clan knew by now, which meant he'd have to talk with Arabella sooner rather than later, before someone tried to congratulate Arabella and catch her off guard.

It was a bloody miracle his family had kept mum about it, probably only because they knew Arabella better than the rest of the clan and knew how uneasy she'd be with another child on the way.

He eyed the Stonefire leader. Apart from his family, Bram was one of the few people he let down his walls around. Running a hand through his hair, he blew out a breath. "Aye. There weren't supposed to be any more bairns, you see. It's my fault she's pregnant this time."

As he explained the situation to Bram, Finn's burden eased a fraction. Regardless of how he poked and prodded the Stonefire leader, he was the best friend a male could have.

Not that he'd voice that out loud, of course.

When he finished, Bram crossed his arms over his chest and studied Finn a second before saying, "I can see why you'd want to wait to discuss it with her, but she's probably just as anxious as you. Talk to her now, Finn. There's nothing planned until tomorrow, after all. And if your family is busy, Evie and I will watch the triplets whilst you two chat."

He raised an eyebrow. "Six children together will give you gray hair, old man."

Bram snorted. "I have a few already, from when Evie gave birth to our daughter. A few more will make me distinguished."

Finn grinned. "Then maybe take the triplets for a week, and that should do it."

Bram shook his head. "Don't push it, Finn." He sobered. "But that's decided—have the triplets brought over and take Ara to one of those pretty beaches you always go on about. It's warm enough today she won't freeze her arse off."

"Don't talk about my mate's arse," he growled.

Bram rolled his eyes. "The sooner you talk to your mate, the better. I most definitely prefer your teasing to crankiness."

His dragon laughed at the description, but Finn ignored him. "Aye, fine. Let's go. Ara and I will drop off the triplets as soon as we can."

And as they chatted a bit more and walked toward the main living area, Finn both looked forward to and dreaded his outing with Arabella.

But he wasn't a coward, and it was time they discussed the latest surprise to pop up into their life. With any luck, it'd be the last one that showed up for a good long while.

ARABELLA HAD BEEN DISCUSSING self-defense training regimes with Delaney Griffiths—the human female had a number of them designed for humans living with dragon-shifters—when first Rhydian, and soon after Finn, unexpectedly showed up earlier than expected.

Once Rhydian had whisked his mate away, and

Arabella was left alone with Finn, she finally asked, "What happened to the clan leader meeting?"

Finn took her hand, brought it to his lips, and kissed it. His warmth helped to relax her a fraction. He finally replied, "We all decided to spend some time with our mates and meet again tomorrow."

Knowing her mate as she did, Arabella sensed it was only part of the truth. "That doesn't go along with the schedule we created for their visit."

He smiled at her, brought her up against his front, and stroked her cheek with the back of his fingers. "No, but sometimes plans change without warning."

Warning bells rang inside her head. Was Finn finally going to bring up her pregnancy, now of all times?

Her dragon murmured, *I think it's time to talk about it.*

*But the other leaders—*

Her beast cut her off. *Will be fine for an afternoon. If Finn's dragon is anything like me, he's fed up with this human way of dealing with it. Just talk to Finn about it. As he's shown over the years, he loves us no matter what.*

"Ara?" At her mate's voice, she focused back on his face, and he continued, "It'll be fine, lass. And Bram's volunteered him and Evie to watch the triplets so we can escape to our favorite beach."

She looked at him askance. "Bram willingly

offered to watch them? He does know they're little terrors at the moment, right?"

Finn snorted. "Only for us. They're wee angels for everyone else, as you well know."

She grunted. "The little traitors."

He continued to stroke her cheek. "You can't fool me, love. You'd miss them if they weren't here."

Sighing, she leaned more against Finn's tall frame. "I know. It's just that when I finally think I have the boys settled, then Freya acts up. And vice versa. It's as if they're trying to drive me mad."

His voice softened as he said, "I've told you before we can get help with the triplets. Kaylee MacDonald works part-time, watching other children on Lochguard. I'm sure she'd come a few hours a day if you needed her."

Arabella trusted the human female—Kaylee's sister was mated to Fergus, who was Finn's cousin— but accepting her help was almost as if Arabella admitted to failure.

She'd started off motherhood well, but day by day, she felt as if any control she had over her children was slipping away.

Although how could she explain it in a way that Finn would understand?

Her beast spoke up. *It's not failure. Any offspring of Finn's would be a handful.*

*True. But the same could be said of any of the children*

*from the MacKenzie brood. And yet they don't seem to have the same problem.*

*Aye, but none of them have three toddler terrors at once.*

*Two of his cousins have twins.*

*Perhaps, but that's still only two bairns and not three at once. And none of them have to deal with a toddler-shifting dragon, either. That would make any of them run for the hills.*

As far as anyone knew, Freya was the only dragon-shifter to be able to shift from almost infancy without going rogue. *Maybe.*

Arabella smiled at the image of all the MacKenzie offspring shifting at once, and Finn raised his brows. She explained, "I was going to refuse, but my dragon reminded me that they are *your* children, after all, which means of course they'll be little hellions."

"So you'll accept some help?"

At the question in Finn's eyes, Arabella nodded. "A little. But only for a trial period, to see how it goes."

Speaking the words and knowing help would be coming forthwith eased the tightness in Arabella's shoulders and neck a fraction.

For two years, she'd tried to do it all on her own. Oh, Finn's family helped sometimes, but Arabella had been determined to be the best mother she could to her triplets. Almost as if to prove to herself that she was strong in a way she hadn't been since before the dragon hunter attack.

But with another child on the way, she couldn't allow herself to be foolish. Yes, she might sometimes lack confidence or struggle with her shyness, but she was definitely not a fool.

Finn kissed her gently and pulled away a fraction to whisper, "Good. Now, help me get the triplets ready to stay with Bram. I need help finding the most irritating toys they have and pack them all."

Arabella laughed. "That's horrible, Finn. He's nice enough to watch our three with his own three. We shouldn't make it worse."

Finn leaned back and winked at her. "He can take the toys away, if it bothers him. But you know he'd try to do the same with me, if I watched his bairns."

She half-heartedly rolled her eyes. "Fine, I'll help pack them. But just remember that payback is a bitch."

"I'll take that under advisement." He took her hand and gently tugged. "Come on. I want to spend as much time alone on the beach with my bonny mate as I can."

At the heated look in his eyes, she blushed.

Soon she forgot about heated glances and helped Finn get Declan, Grayson, and Freya packed up and dropped off with Bram and Evie.

And before she knew it, they were in their dragon forms, gliding toward their favorite beach. For all the rocky, cragginess of Scotland, some of the best beaches had soft, light-colored sand, perfect for enjoying the sunshine.

Her dragon spoke up. *I want to enjoy the sunshine, but I won't doze off until you talk with Finn.*

She mentally sighed. *Fine, I will. Just give me a chance to figure out how to broach the topic.*

*Be direct. That works best with our mate.*

True, but apart from her own doubts, she knew Finn would feel guilt for her pregnancy as well.

Regardless, she couldn't put it off any longer. Arabella wasn't the female who hid away from the world any longer. And it was time she remembered that.

## Chapter Nine

As soon as Finn and Arabella had shifted back to their human forms and tossed on the clothes they'd carried with them—as much as Finn loved his mate's naked body, sand did tend to get *everywhere*—he took her hand and guided her to some rocks situated slightly above the surf. Since it was sunny, they were nice and warm.

Even so, he couldn't resist pulling Arabella close against his side and wrapping his arms around her. Once he laid his cheek against the top of her head, they watched the water tumble forward and back a few times before Arabella sighed and spoke first. "You know, don't you?"

Squeezing her slightly, he answered, "Of course, lass. For weeks now."

Not wanting to push, he was content to hold his mate and watch the waves for about thirty seconds before she finally spoke again. "At first, I panicked. It wasn't something I'd prepared for, even though in the back of my mind I knew it was a possibility."

"Because I failed to keep my promise."

"You didn't do it on purpose, Finn."

With a sigh, he pulled back a fraction and turned his head so he could meet Arabella's brown-eyed gaze. "I still should've been more careful."

"You had been using condoms. I think it was my surprise seduction, that day in and around the lake, when this happened."

She gestured down toward her abdomen, and Finn resisted the urge to put his hand over her belly. "I still could've pulled out to lessen the risk." He paused and added, "Some bloody clan leader I am when I can't even take care of my mate."

Fire flashed in Arabella's eyes. "If I remember correctly—and I do, by the way—I had my legs wrapped around your hips. So pulling out wasn't an option unless you were going to break my legs to do so."

His temper flared a fraction. "Stop trying to absolve me of the blame, Arabella. It's my fault I'm going to put you through hell again."

Her lips thinned, signaling she wasn't going to smile and agree with him. "The pregnancy and birth itself isn't the problem, Finlay. It's what comes after that I worry about."

He frowned. "What are you talking about? My

family—and yours, given your dad is doing so much better these days—are all there to help you when you need it. And this time around, I'll insist you take their help."

"And that, right there, is the bloody problem," she gritted.

He searched her face. "What the hell are you talking about?"

"Putting aside the energy and willpower it takes to deal with *your* offspring, I barely manage things as they are now. Adding another child, and then asking your family's help, will make me look weak and like a bad mother."

Finn blinked, trying to absorb her words.

However, before he could say anything, Arabella continued, "People still tiptoe around me, even after all these years since the dragon hunter attack. And if everyone closes ranks around me at the first sign of weakness to help take care of my youngest child, do you know what'll most likely happen? They'll probably tiptoe around me even more after that, and *that* will be the bloody worst of it."

Aye, Arabella hated pity more than anything.

It was the reason she'd first come to Lochguard, to start over somewhere new, where people didn't treat her like a porcelain doll about to break. Aye, a few people from Lochguard still eyed her that way once they knew her history, but not the majority of the clan.

Maybe if he wasn't already struggling to keep his temper under control, Finn could've thought of a rational response. Instead, he took Arabella by the shoulders, leaned close, and said, "No one on Lochguard thinks you're weak or a bad mother, at least that I know of. And if they've said anything, you'd better tell me, Ara. No more bloody secrets."

Her voice raised an octave. "I wouldn't keep secrets if you didn't overreact. You can't glare and make everything perfect."

"Of course I can."

She rolled her eyes. "No, you can't. I understand you're protective, but I've done so well over the last couple of years, and you had to step in less and less. But with this baby, you're just going to get worse all over again."

He frowned. "All dragonmen are protective of their mates, more so if they're pregnant."

"And I understand that. But don't you see? If you start becoming more overprotective, like early on in our mating, then it'll make me feel like a failure, Finn, more than what anyone else thinks. And I don't want to be a failure."

Her voice cracked on the last few words, breaking through Finn's temper. He cupped her cheek and gentled his voice. "You're not a failure, love. You're one of the strongest people I know."

A tear rolled down her cheek and it was as if someone squeezed his heart with their talons. She whispered, "Not compared to all the other clan leaders' mates."

He desperately hoped Arabella's feelings were heightened because of her pregnancy, but he wasn't going to assume so.

Finn took her face between his hands and waited for her to meet his gaze again. "Why would you say that?"

She bit her lip a second before answering, "They almost all have children and find ways to also help their clan or dragonkind. I barely have time for my children, let alone anything else."

"What rubbish." She narrowed her eyes, but Finn pushed on. "How many times have we needed your hacking skills to help one clan or another?"

"Not often."

"No, only when we desperately needed them to save lives."

"It's not the same, Finn. Not like Delaney with her training regimes or Evie with her work with the DDA. Not to mention Aaron and Caitlin both working for their mates to form stronger alliances between the UK and Ireland."

Finn leaned a fraction closer, determined to make her see what he did. "If not for you, Lochguard and Stonefire wouldn't be as close of allies as they are now."

"That's not true—"

He shook his head. "Aye, it is." He stroked her

cheeks with his thumbs. "You're bloody amazing, Arabella MacLeod. Not just because I somehow convinced you to be my mate and endure the madness of my family, but you're clever. And resilient. And often notice things I miss. I don't care what other clan leaders do with their mates, but I wouldn't be the clan leader I am if not for you. Lochguard is as strong as it is now because you agreed to be more than my mate—you're my partner in all things. And if you don't bloody see that, then I'm going to have to lecture you until you do, Arabella MacLeod."

After a few beats—ones where his heart pounded and his stomach twisted in knots—she finally smiled. "Is 'lecture' code for shouting at me? Because I'd rather avoid that. Your voice gets a little high-pitched when you do."

He grunted. "Now you're just making things up."

"It's the truth, I swear. I think it would make dogs bark, if they heard it."

He battled a smile and lost. If Arabella could tease him, then he must be on the right track. "We'll have to test that hypothesis at some point, lass." He sobered. "But I hope I've convinced you of not only how important you are to me and the clan, but that you're the farthest thing from a failure. If not, I may be tempted to take drastic measures."

She raised a dark eyebrow. "Such as?"

"Tossing you into the sea, to wake you up a wee bit."

"Which is freezing and that can't be good for our baby."

He gave a comical sigh. "Then I'll just have to find another way to get your nipples hard and ready for my mouth."

She lightly hit his shoulder. "You can talk about nipples later."

He purred, "I'd like to do more than talk about them."

"Stop it, Finn."

He winked, but then nodded. "Aye, I'll behave. But I'm still waiting on your answer about how important you are, lass, and that you understand that."

She searched his eyes again. Her pupils flashed a few times before she replied, "I won't outright dismiss it." He opened his mouth to convince her, but she continued, "But for now, I want you to promise me that any decisions regarding our children, extra help, and asking for it will be discussed. You mention how we're a team for the clan, but I think we need to work on that a bit more for our little family. I'll try to accept some more help and you'll work on being less overprotective. Also, you need to try not to spoil the kids as much as you do so that I'm not always the bad guy. Okay?"

For some reason, Finn had never really thought

about how Arabella did most of the scolding or corrections for their children. But thinking a second, it was true.

His poor lass. No wonder she was worried about a fourth bairn.

His dragon grunted. *I think you need to delegate more so you can help our mate.*

*It might be time, dragon. It might be time.*

Finn replied to his mate, "I'll do my best, but it's hard not to spoil our triplets."

"Because you want them to always think kindly about their dad, right?"

He sighed. His mate truly understood him better than anyone. "I don't plan on leaving them or getting killed like what happened with my parents. But even so, I want them to always have fond thoughts of me. That way, they'll never forget me."

"I know, but spoiling them all the time won't help them later in life, Finn. And I don't like being the bloody villain all the time, either." She placed her hand over one of his. "I need you to help, especially with our daughter. She listens to you most of all."

His dragon spoke up again. *She's right. Even I can tell, and dragons don't usually notice such things.*

Arabella lightly squeezed his biceps. "Does your dragon agree with me?"

"Aye, he does, love. And I suppose I could try a little harder. The lads are starting to destroy a lot of things with those wooden sticks of theirs."

She snorted. "Try just about everything at hip level or below. But at least you admit it now." She moved her hand to his cheek. "I really do think that consistency will help tame some of the worst of the destruction."

"Which will then make it less stressful with the new bairn." She nodded, and he kissed her quickly before adding, "Then we'll form a plan together."

She smiled at him, and most of his worries melted away. His mate was never as beautiful as when she smiled.

Och, well, almost never. His favorite was when she was flushed and languid from an orgasm.

His beast growled. *Then hurry up and finish talking so we can claim her.*

Trying not to think of the blanket he'd brought, just in case he could take Arabella on the sand, he focused back on the issue at hand. "Right, so the situation with our current bairns is sorted. But prepare yourself, lass, because I'm going to talk to you all the time about our fourth—and last—bairn to ensure you get the help you need."

"Let's hope it's only one more," she muttered.

"I'm going to hope along with you. And I'm going to talk to Layla and Alex to see if one of them can fit in a vasectomy the day after all the leaders leave. Woe betide any bastard who tries to delay it this time."

"Don't jinx it, Finn."

He leaned closer to his mate's face and nuzzled her cheek. "Even if Bram has to stay and bloody take charge for a day, there won't be any more delays. I vow it, Ara."

She bobbed her head, and he kissed just below her ear. He asked, "And we can wait as long as you like to officially announce you're pregnant, although the entire clan probably knows by now."

"It's extremely inconvenient that every dragon male can tell already."

He snorted. "It just guarantees we can protect our mates."

"Overprotect them, you mean."

Finn leaned back. "I already said I'd try to be better. What else can I do to prove it?"

She ran a hand down his chest and back up, until she traced the edge of his jaw. "Well, if you take me hard on this beach, it might just show how you don't think I'll break."

"And my little seductress is emerging again. I have to admit, I like her."

Her hand traveled back down his chest and further still, until she could cup his cock and balls. Even through the fabric of his trousers, he instantly hardened.

She murmured, "I was usually sick when pregnant with the triplets, but this time around, I'm fairly randy." She gave a coy look. "Do you think you can help with that?"

With a growl, he took her mouth with his. As his tongue stroked, and explored, and devoured the silkiness of her mouth, he let her know just how much he still wanted her.

And it didn't take him long to strip away their clothes, hastily toss down the blanket, and take Arabella hard from behind.

Then he took her laying down, and eventually also sitting on his lap.

Aye, by the time the sun started to sink toward the sea, his mate said he'd convinced her that she wouldn't break. He'd just have to ensure she felt that way every day of her pregnancy and beyond.

## Chapter Ten

It was the day before the final celebration of the week-long gathering when Evie Marshall finally managed to get all the clan leader mates together in one of the meeting rooms of Lochguard's great hall.

Well, most of them. She'd debated including Honoria and Asher, but since this meeting took place during the same time as the clan leader one, Evie had decided to leave them out this time. After all, their situation was a bit different.

And if today went well, then Evie would make this sort of thing a regular occurrence at the twice-yearly clan gatherings. She could corner the Skyhunter pair in the future.

As she watched the last person to arrive—Aaron —enter and sit down, a somewhat wary glance on his face, she resisted a chuckle.

He was, after all, the only man in the room. But

if he had been Teagan's mate this long, then he had to be comfortable with the unusual role reversals for most dragon-shifters.

Evie locked the door before moving back to the front of the room and clapped her hands to get started. "Right, well, it seems we're all here now. Thanks for coming. I wasn't sure if we'd manage it or not, since it wasn't on the itinerary."

Arabella raised her brows. "You could've asked me to include it, Evie."

She shrugged. "To be honest, I hadn't planned on anything like this until the last few days. But over the course of this week, between chatting with everyone and observing, I noticed a pattern, one we need to work on."

Aaron cleared his throat. "And what's that?"

Never one to beat around the bush, she stated, "All of our mates work too much."

Evie noticed Delaney was the first to glance around the room. As the newest clan leader mate out of them all—not to mention the only other human in the room besides herself—Evie sensed the woman was a little hesitant.

But if so, Delaney obviously pushed past it and said, "Aye, that's true, they do. But I'm not sure what we can do about it. I pester Rhydian to let me help him, but he says he can do it and not to worry. I'm sure he's not the only stubborn arse amongst the lot, either."

Aaron sighed. "No, he's not. Teagan's the same. And in her case, it's even worse because she has to prove herself twice as much as a male."

Evie felt for Teagan's situation and the need to reach unattainable standards, but she still thought the dragonwoman could do with some extra help, all without losing the respect of her clan. "Regardless, *all* of our mates think they have to do everything. It took me years to get Bram to delegate even a little, and it's still not enough. But…"

Caitlin asked, "But what?"

She grinned. "If we join forces, well, then we might have a stronger chance at succeeding."

Arabella frowned. "And can we do that and have it work?" She gestured toward each person in turn. "Each of us have different situations. A blanket approach won't work to fix them all."

Evie stood tall and stated, "Maybe not, but a general game plan will." The other four people in the room all looked at each other, but Evie pushed on. "We all know how dragon-shifters take their vows seriously, to the point they'll often die to maintain them. Well, we'll use that to our advantage. I say we hole up here, keep the door locked, and only let them in if they vow to delegate some tasks to others. That way they can spend one full evening a week with their families, uninterrupted save for some sort of catastrophe."

Aaron snorted. "Are you sure that will work?"

Evie raised an eyebrow. "Has Teagan ever broken one of her vows before?"

The dragonman paused and then shook his head. "Not since I've met her."

She nodded. "Exactly. I'm sure less honorable dragon-shifters break them without thought, but all of our mates aren't those kind of people. Men and women who will give their lives to protect their clan, no matter what, tend to view honor quite highly."

Delaney asked, "But even if they agree, what about my sons? I can't just abandon them for who knows how long it gets them to agree. I don't know all of your mates very well, but mine is rather stubborn."

Everyone in the room chuckled, but Evie explained to the newest clan leader mate, "Delaney, they all are stubborn arses. But I think so are we. It usually takes one to deal with a clan leader."

The human woman looked around the room. "Doesn't that mean we'll just sit here forever at an impasse? If it were just me, I wouldn't care. But my oldest son will start to worry and will probably plan a rescue attempt."

Evie smiled at the thought of the boy trying to outmaneuver all the dragon clan leaders to get them out of this room. "Don't worry about the children. I already asked all those watching them right now to be on hand, in case this lasts a while. Think of it as a big slumber party, where all the children can interact with one another. Most of them are quite young, but it never hurts to start forming bonds, right?"

Delaney looked unconvinced. But before she could say anything, Arabella reached over and touched the woman's hand. "I think most of our mates already know they work too much. This might just be the extra little push they need to finally admit it out loud. In my opinion, it won't take long. At least my mate won't let it go on long, trust me."

Caitlin spoke up before anyone else could get a word in. "I should mention something now, about Lorcan, since your wee plan won't really affect him." Evie frowned, but Caitlin continued before she could ask a question. "Lorcan's sharing with the others during today's meeting that he's retiring by the end of the month. He won't be clan leader much longer."

After a split second, Evie's pushed aside her shock and curiosity. She'd find out about the new Northcastle leader from her mate once she finished this. "Even so, maybe you being here can help Aaron persuade your daughter to agree. She's probably going to be the longest to hold out, given what I've heard."

Aaron and Caitlin shared a glance, but it was Caitlin who spoke again. "I can try. But you're right —if Teagan's not careful, she's going to work herself to death trying to change the mind of the old timers who think a female should never be clan leader."

Muttering something Evie couldn't hear, Aaron merely nodded.

Two down, two to go, then.

Evie looked at Arabella. "Are you with us?"

She shrugged. "Since there's a toilet through that door, I'm fine. Even this early in my pregnancy, I have to pee all the time."

Evie had wondered when Arabella would say something. They all knew she was pregnant again, but thankfully they all treated it as nothing so that the little meeting didn't get derailed. They could celebrate Finn and Arabella's news later, just like Lorcan's.

Evie nodded. "Right, then we have one last person." She glanced to Delaney, hoping all her arguments had worked. Evie knew the other human the least, and given how Delaney had been surrounded only by Clan Snowridge for over a year now, she might not feel comfortable standing up against her mate. "Delaney, what about you?"

The human woman sat up straight and tossed her long black hair over her shoulder. "You've convinced me, so count me in. I'd hoped this trip would show Rhydian how Carys and Wren are more than willing to help him out more. But maybe this stunt will be the extra bit he needs to finally take the leap, aye?"

Evie grinned and looked at everyone around the room in turn. "Brilliant. Now, we just need to send text messages about us holing up here, and why, and then wait for them to come growling and shouting for us to come out, thinking somehow that will work."

As everyone chuckled—a clear sign that they knew dragon-shifter leaders well—they all went to work sending the notes to their mates and making their demand.

She did feel a tiny bit guilty since Bram had tried to delegate more, but what with the three children now, and the ramping up of the dragon hunters again, she didn't want to take any chances.

So she went to work on her note. If this worked, then she would definitely get the clan leader mates together again to do more. Maybe a project or some sort of campaign.

But first and foremost—it was time to help their mates find a better work-life balance.

For all the good Rhydian had experienced during his time on Lochguard, Delaney's recent text message and demands almost made him regret bringing his mate to Scotland.

As he followed Finn and the other leaders down a hallway inside the great hall, his dragon spoke up. *It's not that big of a deal. It's just what she's been asking for months now—to lean more on those you trust on Snowridge.*

*It's more than that, dragon, and you know it. I've barely gotten the clan to accept her and the idea of more humans, and now she wants me to delegate and all but announce to the clan that I can't handle matters.*

Before his beast could reply, Finn stopped in front of a door and banged on it. "Let me in, Ara."

The female barely said, "Not until you agree to my request," before Rhydian pushed his way to the front. He knew his mate wasn't the only one pregnant inside that room, but Delaney was human. And if she missed her scheduled dragon's blood shot in a few hours, he didn't want to think of how it increased her risk of dying.

He tried the doorknob, but it was locked, of course. Not caring if all the leaders were watching him, he kicked the door inward, busting it open, and he strolled into the room. He found Delaney's gaze and stated, "What were you thinking?"

His female tipped her nose in the air, and Rhydian ignored his dragon's groan at what was coming.

Especially when she crossed her arms over her chest, a sure sign that she wasn't happy. "I'm merely trying to help you, you bastard. And what do you do with my help? Why you break down the bloody door like an eejit."

Not caring that his audience had now doubled with the leaders' mates in the room, Rhydian took a step closer toward Delaney and grunted. "I'd do it a million times more if it meant getting you out of here and to the doctor, as you're supposed to."

Delaney rolled her eyes. "I had my last shot a few weeks ago. I'm not even late for the appointment, and even if I was, a few hours difference won't kill me."

After he'd mated Delaney, Rhydian had researched as much as he could about human-female-and-dragon-male pairings. Some of the horrors of their deaths—both during pregnancy and the birth—had steeled his resolve to protect Delaney as much as possible.

His first solution had been to not have any more children after Damien.

However, Delaney wasn't having that. She wanted a big family, and much to his chagrin, the wily minx had easily seduced him into agreeing for as many as she wanted.

But if they were to have more kids, then he'd vowed to give her as much dragon's blood as necessary to help her survive.

And she'd agreed never to miss an appointment, barring some sort of disaster or catastrophe.

Neither of which suited the current situation.

Rhydian tried to round the table to get to her, but the other mates closed ranks around her, with the dragonman, Aaron, in front.

As he tried to think of a way to get Delaney out of the room without killing any of the others helping her, Bram laid a hand on his shoulder, garnering his attention. The Stonefire leader said, "I, out of all the others, understand your fears, Rhydian, since my mate is also human and I went through the same thing. But she's right—a few hours or even a day one way or the other won't affect her treatment or decrease her chances of survival."

Part of him knew that. But Rhydian hadn't fought for the first human female he'd fancied years ago, long before he'd met Delaney, and had vowed to never be such a coward again.

Keeping his gaze trained on his mate, he replied, "Her text said she'd stay here for as long as possible, and I won't risk it. I won't risk her."

Delaney's gaze softened a fraction. "And you won't. But don't you see? How you feel right now is how I feel all the time. No, you can't die from pregnancy or childbirth, but you can from working yourself to death." She walked toward him, pushing past the others until she could lay a hand on his cheek, the one with his scars, and lightly caressed his skin. "All we want is to ensure you lot enjoy some downtime, to help with your stress levels and be pains in our arses for decades to come."

Before he could reply, Aaron walked over to Teagan and said, "Which is twice as hard on you, love, what with being able to get pregnant *and* having the burden of a clan leader. Keep going as you are, and I'm afraid Kelly and I will lose you all too soon."

Delaney continued to stroke Rhydian's cheek and cleared her throat, catching his attention again. She said, "You have to admit it's been nice spending time with me and the lads this week, Rhydian. Imagine being able to do that a bit more, aye?"

His dragon spoke up. *We've done the hard work of ferreting out the unsympathetic back home. Giving more duties to Carys and Wren wouldn't hurt.*

*So now I have both of you working against me?*

*For your own good, yes.*

Even as all the mates murmured between each other, Rhydian didn't move his gaze from Delaney. "I'll try, but that's all I can promise right now."

She looped her arms around his neck and leaned against him, her scent and heat helping to calm him down further. "I'll hold you to it. Otherwise, I'll have to try locking myself up and sending a message again until you agree."

He raised his brows. "You did see me kick in that door, didn't you?"

The corner of her mouth kicked up. "Well, the good thing about Snowridge is that it's mostly inside the mountains. I'm sure I can reinforce a door, and you can't burst through a solid wall of rock without bringing down who knows how many rooms and living quarters."

He wrapped his arms around her waist and leaned his head down a fraction closer to hers. "Maybe there are secret tunnels you don't know about."

"Are there?"

He grinned. "I'm not telling."

Before his mate could argue more, he kissed her. Even now, when she was trying to stand up for him and make him see some sense—yes, sense, although Rhydian wasn't about to admit it just yet—she opened and allowed him to lick, and nibble, and caress her mouth and lips until they were both breathless. When he finally broke away, they both breathed heavily and stared at one another with heated gazes.

Delaney murmured, "So if you agree to ask for help once we get home, I may just reward you a little."

He nuzzled her cheek. "Is that so?"

"A few others have already left to do so with their own mates."

A quick glance told him that he and Delaney, as well as Teagan and Aaron, were the only ones still left in the room. "I do think we have an hour or so before you're due to see Dr. McFarland. That should be a good appetizer for what I have planned for later."

"Later, huh?"

He scooped Delaney into his arms and carried her right out of the room. "Tonight is the last full night we have here, without any engagements. So yes, I plan to make the most of it."

And Rhydian did exactly that, teasing his mate until she cried out his name several times.

## Chapter Eleven

The following evening, Arabella's face hurt from smiling so much.

Finn had insisted that the two of them greeted everyone who came in, which also implied she needed to be a slightly more charming female than normal, to be the best hostess.

Not that Arabella didn't like to smile sometimes, but she wasn't a charmer like her mate. Talking with so many people and trying to be cheery for an extended period of time drained her like nothing else.

Well, almost. Thoughts of Finn taking her on the beach flashed inside her mind.

Her dragon laughed. *We should do that more often. Finn said he'd help with our randiness as much as needed.*

*Of course he did,* Arabella replied dryly.

As she glanced up at Finn and he quickly winked

at her, her cheeks flushed. She rather looked forward to everyone leaving the next day and she and Finn having one last afternoon to spend naked together before his scheduled vasectomy.

Yet as much as letting her male recover would be hard, she would be relieved beyond measure. Well, almost as much as when they could find out in a few weeks if they were having one or multiples.

*Please let it only be one*, she mentally pleaded.

As the last couple left them and went to find their spots inside the great hall, Arabella sighed. "I didn't think Aimee would come, but I was hoping maybe she'd take up the offer to dine in one of the rooms on the first floor, overlooking the room, to be tangentially included."

Finn wrapped an arm around her waist and guided her toward the front, where all the clan leaders and their families sat. "Someday, love. She'll be ready someday."

Arabella nodded and merely took a few seconds of comfort from her mate's touch before Finn helped her sit, and he went to the stage. When he whistled, the room quieted. Well, as much as it ever did on Lochguard, which was to say a few people continued to chat in whispers.

But since the culprits were Meg Boyd and her two paramours, Finn ignored them, knowing full well Meg would cause a fuss over nothing, like she always did, if he singled her out.

Finn finally spoke. "Thank you all for coming tonight. Lochguard has made our visitors welcome, and you should all be proud." Some cheers went up before it quieted again. "Important business was discussed, of course, but we've also come up with a number of ways for our clans to become better acquainted. To that end, we're going to continue the tradition of gathering together on other clan lands. The next gathering will be held on Stonefire, and in addition to the leaders, a few individuals from each clan will also be selected to go. Details on how you can be included will be forthcoming in the next few weeks.

"But all of that is in the future. For tonight, let's celebrate and show our guests that Lochguard knows how to have a grand time, aye?"

Cheers went up again, and Finn grinned before descending to the floor and taking his seat next to Arabella.

As soon as he did, Bram spoke up. "You've done a good job, but it's now my goal to outshine you in every way for the gathering on Stonefire."

Arabella rolled her eyes, but Finn, of course, wouldn't let it lie. "You can try, but Stonefire is a much stuffier lot, aye? I doubt the other leaders and their families will be laughing as much as they have here."

Bram shrugged. "I don't think they're laughing

out of joy. More like they're annoyed but being polite."

Evie caught Arabella's eyes and rolled her own before they grinned at one another.

It seemed their mates were back to bickering.

Not that Arabella minded. She had friends—both old and new—surrounding her, and she could let her mate tease Bram for as long as he wanted.

Ignoring the two males, Arabella turned and chatted with Delaney on her other side, and Caitlin and Aaron and Evie and even Honoria, when she could. Really, they should've put the clan leader mates together.

Watching everyone talk, and laugh, and have a good time made Arabella's heart soar. Not only had Lochguard's inaugural hosting gone well, but things were also back to normal with her mate. And as a boon, she'd made new friends who knew the strains and trials only a clan leader's mate could truly understand.

Going forward, they were going to rely a lot more on each other to both help when needed and work together to ensure the best future for their clans and families.

Everything was so different compared to a few years ago, when Arabella had been alone and isolated. But she looked forward to the future and how much closer the dragon clans could be.

## Epilogue

*A few weeks later*

F inn sat next to Arabella, who was half laying on the examination table as Logan Lamont moved the ultrasound wand against her lower abdomen.

Both he and Arabella waited with bated breath to hear if they were having just one bairn this time or more.

For Arabella's sake, he hoped only one.

His dragon spoke up. *No matter how many bairns, we're going to help more. That way Ara won't be so stressed.*

*Aye, but one would be the easiest. And after everything we've been through since becoming clan leader, it'd be nice to have something go our way for once.*

His beast snorted as Finn tried to make sense of

the image on the screen. But it looked like a lot of blobs of nothing to him.

Finally Logan pressed a button, freezing the image, and smiled at them as he pointed to a section of the screen. "See here—just the one this time, aye?"

They both let out a collective sigh of relief.

Between the revelation they were only having one child and that Finn had finally gone through with his vasectomy, he hoped Arabella's worries were finally over. At least for the foreseeable future.

Logan cleaned his instrument and Arabella's belly before he stood and smiled at them. "I'll give you two a few minutes alone. Everything looks good to me, but Dr. McFarland will come double-check, just to make sure."

With that, the nurse left, and Finn finally looked into Arabella's eyes. She smiled at him and squeezed his hand in hers. "Just the one, Finn. I can handle that, I think."

Since Kaylee had been hired to help with the triplets a few hours a day, several times a week, Arabella had smiled more. Not to mention she had also focused some of her free time on video conferences with the other clan leader mates—plus Honoria Wakeham—planning who the bloody hell knew what.

But it made his mate happy, and that was all that mattered to Finn. "Aye, one more. Although now comes the waiting to see if it's a lad or lassie."

"If it's a boy, poor Freya. Three brothers, even if one will be younger, will probably push her to rebel to no end, once she's older."

Finn worried the most about his daughter getting into trouble someday, but right here, right now, he wasn't going to fret over it. He'd have plenty of time in the future to get gray hairs.

Instead, he brought Arabella's hand to his lips and kissed it. "She'll have her female cousins at her back, including Fraser's twins, who are supposed to save the bloody world, or some such shite."

Twin female dragon-shifters were rare, to the point legends had sprung up around them. Each previous pair had supposedly done heroic things. The twins' father liked to crow about it as often as possible.

Arabella snorted. "We'll see. Their mother is very much no-nonsense. Holly won't let it go to their heads."

He raised an eyebrow. "But their father? You know Fraser, and he's the worst when it comes to stirring up trouble, aye?" He brushed back a few stray strands of Arabella's dark hair away from her face and murmured, "But enough about all the other bairns. I think I need some more lessons about how to scold our own." He lowered his voice further. "Private ones."

Arabella rolled her eyes. "Us taking turns to do mock discipline is *not* how it works with children."

His lips twitched. "But it's so much fun when I can spank you for being naughty."

His mate's cheeks flushed pink. "Finn, Layla will be here any second."

"I'm thinking about after."

Before his mate could pretend to resist—he knew she wanted to be whisked away for their free afternoon together—Dr. Layla McFarland walked in and chatted about the ultrasound.

And once she finished, Finn did indeed take his mate somewhere private and celebrated one of the many side benefits to the gathering they'd held—he now had more time to spend with his mate.

## Author's Note

So you may have noticed how this novella is sort of unique in that it features updates from so many different characters, all while revolving around a basic event. I wish I could claim to be the genius who thought up this sort of approach, but I'm not. I love to read as much as write and one of my favorite authors, Grace Callaway (she writes super steamy historical romance with lots of mystery), wrote a novella featuring so many previous characters from her whole universe and a lightbulb went off. In the past, I'd written follow-up novellas featuring one couple. And as much as readers love them, it can be hard to think of an interesting enough one-off story to write 20k+ words without making it feel forced or cheesy. This sort of set up, though, like what I had in *Summer at Lochguard*, makes that so much easier to accomplish since I have tons of characters to use!

Readers get to revisit their favorite couples and I get to play with them all in a win-win situation. I will write at least one more—*Winter at Stonefire*—which will give us another update on Kai and Jane, along with little snippets of other favorite couples. However, further novellas like this depend entirely on my readers. If no one buys them, then I'll have to focus my efforts elsewhere. :)

And don't worry, you'll get updates on Finn and Arabella throughout the Lochguard Highland Dragons series, as usual. Will they have another boy or girl? I already know, but you'll just have to wait and find out. ;)

As always, I have some people to thank in helping me to get this out into the world:

- Becky and her team at Hot Tree Editing are fantastic. It's hard to believe we've been a team for seven years now, but I can't imagine it any other way.
- My betas, as always, are so helpful in finding minor inconsistencies and typos. (Example: They're still naked here, and here, and here. Shouldn't they be dressed by now? LOL.) Huge thanks to Sabrina D., Iliana G., and Sandy H. These ladies are amazing.

As I'm not entirely sure of when *Winter at Stonefire* will be out (probably in 2023 since Stonefire #15 comes before it, timeline-wise), you can always keep updated on release dates by visiting my website at: www.JessieDonovan.com.

Thanks for reading and I hope to see you at the end of the next book!

# Also by Jessie Donovan

*The Heir* (KRW #3)

*The Forbidden* (KRW #4)

*The Hidden* (KRW #5)

*The Survivor* (KRW #6)

## Lochguard Highland Dragons

*The Dragon's Dilemma* (LHD #1)

*The Dragon Guardian* (LHD #2)

*The Dragon's Heart* (LHD #3)

*The Dragon Warrior* (LHD #4)

*The Dragon Family* (LHD #5)

*The Dragon's Discovery* (LHD #6)

*The Dragon's Pursuit* (LHD #7)

*The Dragon Collective* (LHD #8)

*The Dragon's Chance* (LHD # 9)

*The Dragon's Memory* / Emma & Logan (LHD #10 / May 5, 2022)

## Love in Scotland

*Crazy Scottish Love* (LiS #1)

*Chaotic Scottish Wedding* (LiS #2)

## Stonefire Dragons

*Sacrificed to the Dragon* (SD #1)

*Seducing the Dragon* (SD #2)

## WRITING AS LIZZIE ENGLAND

### <u>Her Fantasy</u>

# About the Author

Jessie Donovan has sold over half a million books, has given away hundreds of thousands more to readers for free, and has even hit the *NY Times* and *USA Today* bestseller lists. She is best known for her dragon-shifter series, but also writes about vampires, magic users, aliens, and even has a crazy romantic comedy series set in Scotland. When not reading a book, attempting to tame her yard, or traipsing around some foreign country on a shoestring, she can often be found interacting with her readers on Facebook. She lives near Seattle, where, yes, it rains a lot but it also makes everything green.

Visit her website at: www.JessieDonovan.com